Come Day
—Go Day

John O'Connor Writing School
Armagh City
Co. Armagh

First published by Golden Eagle Books, Dublin, 1948 Facsimile
edition by Blackstaff Press, Belfast, 1984
Limited edition published, Armagh, 2016
Reprinted in 2017

Design: Fergal Condon
fergalcondon@gmail.com
Typset in Palatino

This publication is produced with financial assistance from the
Arts Council of Northern Ireland

Come Day —Go Day

John O'Connor

Foreword

John O'Connor, in the words of his fellow novelist Sam Hanna Bell, was an author who was 'forever writing out of himself, out of his own secret knowledge'. One source of that secret knowledge was O'Connor's childhood in the Mill Row, a cluster of workers' houses huddled in the shadow of the Drumcairn Spinning Mill on the outskirts of Armagh. And it is the Mill Row that provides the setting for O'Connor's only novel, *Come Day – Go Day*, first published by Dublin's Golden Eagle Books in 1948.

When it was republished by Blackstaff Press in 1984, the back cover blurb called *Come Day – Go Day* a 'gentle, evocative novel'; but evocative though it certainly is, there's nothing gentle about this book or the world it depicts. Though there is warmth in its portrayal of this small community, with neighbours juking in and out of one another's houses, the novel is fierce and unflinching in its attention to the underlying harshness of these lives, the constant struggle to keep body and soul together in the face of elemental forces – both the rain that continually threatens to flood the houses, and the Mill that both holds out and withholds the promise of stability.

O'Connor's background as a short story writer is evident throughout, so much so that the novel can read less like a unified narrative than a series of acutely observed episodes. But what might be sacrificed in terms of narrative drive is made up for by the forensic detail of the writing and O'Connor's feel for the textures of family life: its warmth, intimacies and sudden violence.

The line by line writing too is rich and assured: from O'Connor's vivid neologisms – hot water 'japping' out of the spout of a kettle, teeth 'scringing' against a bitter taste – to his unerring ear for the rhythms of everyday speech – 'Thon's a shocking place got altogether.' His characterisation meanwhile is sharp and sensitive. Take for instance new mother Teasie, hounded by the scolding presence of her mother-in-law and belittled by her own weak-willed husband. What seems at first almost like a portrait of post-natal depression reaches a peak of intensity in the extraordinary chapter eight, which plays out like an inverted small-town Irish *Doll's House*: ordinary life as tragedy.

If this combination of the intimate and the epic puts one in mind of other great Irish short story writers of the mid-century – including John O'Connor's namesake Frank – his is a distinctively Northern voice: indeed the novel's setting in the industrial edgelands of a small town brings to mind other, later Northern writers, albeit from the North of England: Alan Sillitoe, say, or Barry Hines.

For this is as much an urban as a rural novel. The characters live in an in-between place, cheek by jowl with the Asylum, the inmates of which become figures of both fun and fear for the children of the Row. Turn one way and you're in town, with its cinemas and fish and chip shops and pubs; turn the other and you're in the country, with the river and the cow fields and the wild shamrock. This urban/rural bifocalism is part of a system of dualities at work in the book. Another is the local versus the wider world.

Though the focus of the novel is tight and intent – one small community on the edge of one small town – there are glimpses of further horizons. Uncle Pachy has spent seven years serving in the British Army in India, and young Neilly and his friends are entranced by the cinema, especially the exploits of Western heroes like Tom Mix and Ken Maynard. So while the loyalties of the characters tend to be local – 'Show us what the ould Row's made of' they urge their bullet-throwing champion, Macklin – the wider world is never far away.

And it was this wider world that exerted a pull on John O'Connor, drawing him away from Ireland in 1952, first to England and ultimately to Australia, where he died in Townsville, Queensland, in 1959, of peritonitis. He was only thirty-nine.

We do not know if he was still writing in those last years. A late letter to Sam Hanna Bell hints at a book of travel writing. But nothing survives. We are left with a couple of dozen short stories, some journalism and radio scripts – and this one novel. This gem of a book.

Daragh Carville
Birkbeck, University of London

Part I

1

'Malachey! Malachey!'

Mrs Coyle's voice stole softly up the dark stairs. In the back room, Neilly, lying scratching an itchy shinbone with the heel of his right foot, suddenly stretched both legs straight and listened intently for his father's answering grunt.

Seconds passed, and then his mother, with urgent sibilance, called again. Neilly heard the bed creak in the front room, and his father's 'Aye, all right!' sounded, clotted with sleep.

'It's ten to eight, Malachey; I'm away!' Mrs Coyle's voice lowered slightly now that her husband was awake. 'Tell them to put their ould clothes on them today. It's still teeming out of the heavens.' There was a soft scuffle of shoes, and then the sound of the front-door latch being lifted. 'And, Malachey, the milk's in the crock down the hall. Don't use up all the potato bread; there's any amount of soda farls in the press.'

The bed in the front room creaked again.

'Aye, all right, all right!'

The front door clashed. Neilly strained his ears after the quick clack-clack of his mother's footsteps. When the sound had died, he still could hear it in his mind, coupled with the vision of his mother crossing the street at the top of the Row, and breasting her way round the Corner, through the swirls of rain.

Now that she had gone, a heavy silence settled over the house. From the kitchen downstairs, came the almost inaudible rustling of the freshly lighted fire, and the sharp, faint pinpoints of sound as the flames began fingering the dry slack; from Neilly's younger brother beside him, and from Eugene in the other bed, issued the soft hustle of their breathing.

Outside, the deep Sunday-morning stillness was beginning to lift, as other people, too, hurried to Chapel.

Somewhere up the street, between the opening and shutting of a door, the shrill bawling of a child gushed out; the wail guillotined abruptly as the door slapped again. Up at the Corner, Keenan's old hound gave a heartbroken growl. Through all ran the whisper-whisper of the rain, remote, impersonal, and yet to Neilly, lying in the silence and semi-darkness, somehow vaguely sinister.

He hunched up his knees and folded his arms across his chest. It would soon be time to get up. His father would not lie in much longer, in case someone would be wanting something from the shop. It wasn't usually that anyone came in for anything on Sunday morning so early, but you never could tell. He began lowering and raising his knees – this was a rugged mountain in the Himalayas; he parted his knees and let the bedclothes sag down – now it had twin peaks. He straightened his legs, and the bed quilt became a trackless desert across which he stumbled, lost, and dying horribly from thirst.

He gave a startled gasp as Shemie's elbow dunted sharply against his ribs.

'Quit it, boy!' Shemie cried. 'I'll tell my father you won't let me sleep.'

For a moment Neilly lay speechless with rage. Then he screwed round fiercely.

'I'll put your eye in a sling if you do that again, you wee Judas ye.'

Shemie did not say anything.

'Hi! You can't sleep any more, boy,' Neilly ordered. 'You have to go up for school.'

Shemie did not answer. He lay on his left side away from Neilly, facing the wall, with only a few matted tangles of hair visible above the quilt.

'D'ye hear me?' Neilly persisted. 'We'll be slapped.'

Like a little eel, Shemie twisted suddenly and gave Neilly a vicious left-hander in the side, at the same time lashing out with both feet in quick succession.

'Now maybe you'll leave me alone,' he cried.

'Neilly, are you at it again in there?' came their father's angry voice.

'Ah, I wasn't doing anything. This wee sphinx here, you can't look at him. He's only after giving me a big dunt in the side.'

'Neilly, if I have to rise up out of this bed this morning, you'll cry "Sorry, am I." That's all, now, I'm telling you.'

There was silence again for a few moments. Neilly lay burning with rage and self-pity. Then he saw Eugene, across in the other bed, trail the clothes from over his eyes.

'What's the matter?' his brother hissed. 'D'ye want to get my father's crab out this morning again?'

Neilly grimaced. 'Ah-h-h-h!' He yawned, and raised himself on his elbow. 'Eugene! Eugene! Can I come over?'

'Aye, come on if you like,' Eugene answered shortly. 'You'd think that you were doing it on purpose, so you would,' he harped at Neilly, as the younger boy crushed in beside him. 'You know as well as I do what my father's like on a Sunday morning. What do you have to start him for?'

'Ah! That wee spider over there! I'll give him what he's not looking for one of these days –'

'It's fairly coming down outside,' Neilly went on after a few moments. 'D'ye hear it? This rain! We hardly got out of the house all day yesterday with it. I bet you the river'll be over its banks. D'ye have to go to work this morning, Eugene?'

Eugene was a telegram boy, and every third Sunday morning he had to go on duty, in turn with the two other young fellows.

'Ah, give my head peace.' Eugene's voice came blurred, his mouth screwed against the pillow. 'You know rightly I would have had to ha' been up long ago if I had to go on today. You do ask some silly questions.'

'How do you sleep in this bed, Eugene?' Neilly unconcernedly went on, gouging his shoulders into the mattress. 'It's terrible lumpy.' He sat up and hammered at it with his fist.

'What do you think you're doing?' Eugene growled, squinting irritably round at him. 'Why can't you lie at rest? This is the last time you're getting in here. Quit that hammering. My father'll hear you.'

Neilly gave the mattress a final belt.

'I think that's all right now,' he said, and lay back for a few moments in silence. Then he said: 'Eugene, are you going out to the bullets after dinner?'

Eugene groaned. 'My God, does your tongue never cease? I might and I mightn't.'

Neilly said nothing, and then Eugene turned over on his back. He wiped the sleep-damp from his eyes, and folded his hands behind his head.

'Anyway,' he muttered, 'there'll be no bullet match today if this rain doesn't stop. You couldn't go out in that.'

'Will you ask my mother if I can go with you, Eugene? She'll let me go if you ask her. Will you?'

In the other bed Shemie sat up suddenly.

'Eugene! Will you ask her to let me come too? Eugene!'

'Ah! You can go with yourself, tell-tale,' Neilly hissed. 'Nobody's taking you.'

'Ah! Let him come, sure, if he wants to,' Eugene said. 'None of you will be allowed, anyway, in that rain.'

Shemie slid out of bed and came tiptoeing across.

'Let's in, Neilly,' he entreated. 'Go on!'

Their father's bed creaked ominously in the next room. Eugene sat up quickly.

'There's my father getting up. Get back quick.'

Ah, let's in, let's in!' Shemie wrenched desperately at the bedclothes. But Neilly held on grimly.

'You're not getting in, I'm telling you.'

From the other room there came the scuffle of bare feet on the boards, and the rasp of a drawer being jerked open. In one movement, and with amazing speed, Shemie hopped back into his own bed, and hauled the clothes over his head.

The room door opened, and their father came out, clad in a pair of navy-blue trousers and a thick, woollen, long-sleeved undershirt. He was of middle height, around forty, and had a heavy limp in his right leg.

'Come on, you two, and don't have me to call you twice.'

Shemie hopped out and Neilly followed.

'Why can't you stay in your own bed, boy?' his father growled, 'instead of hopping about all over the place. Don't let me hear you barking the morrow or the next day, that's all. What are you doing, Eugene? Are you getting up for ten?'

'Ah, I think I'll wait till half-eleven, father,' Eugene answered, 'of a morning like that.'

'Ah, Eugene, come on down,' Neilly pleaded. Things didn't get so bad on a Sunday morning if Eugene was down too.

For answer, Eugene only waved his fingers mockingly at him over the top of the quilt.

Malachey limped slowly down the stairs, holding on to the banisters. Neilly and Shemie followed silently, round the counter and over to the blazing fire. Their hearts were heavy because now there would be no Eugene to share their burden, if their father happened to get his rag out.

The kitchen was small, and made even smaller by the broad counter. This was painted red and, on the side facing the banisters, it was worn and scuffed by the dunts from the customers' knees and boots. The top was covered with blue-checked oilcloth, and held three bottles of mineral water (the middle one, lemon soda, almost empty), a ribbed tumbler and a pair of scales, the yellow chipped weights neatly pyramided on the small pan. Between the end of the counter, which also served as a cupboard, and the banisters, was a heavy red screen hanging from brass rings, and reaching almost to the floor. At the top end of the counter there was a thin partition, with narrow shelves, stocked with an assortment of goods – tins of Brasso, salve and polish; bottles of Brillantine; cough medicine and Neave's food; boxes of matches; cards of segs, with other odds and ends. A glossy mane of boot laces hung high up, just within arm's length.

On another shelf, across the window, were three bottles of sweets, and below them more sweets were laid out in boxes; jujubes, liquorice allsorts, caramels and a treacle toffee. Between the bottles and the boxes dangled a large card of Mrs Cullen's headache powders; strung across the clean lace curtains, to protect them where one's hand reached through for the confectionery, was a strip of blue satin.

Malachey lifted the kettle from the hob and hung it on the hook over the fire. The water, already warm, began to hum, and the tiny soot flakes on the kettle quivered and fluttered in the thrust of the flames. He sat down in the armchair, and pulled his clean socks from the line above the fire.

'Your mother left word for you two to put your old clothes on today,' he ordered, and no dilly-dallying either. I'm not in very good order this morning, I'm telling you.'

In an effort to spread goodwill and start off on the right foot, Shemie said pleasantly: 'Will we keep on these ould shirts too, Da?'

'No, you'll not keep on these ould shirts too, Da! Man, but you're a through-other being. What's those hanging in front of your eyes?'

Neilly made a sideways grimace at his brother. Feeling rather subdued, the boys pulled their shirts off and took the clean ones from the line.

'Did you change your semmits?'

'Yes.' They nodded eagerly, glad to be able to give the right answer. 'Last night before we went to bed.'

'Ah! It's a wonder you done that much itself.'

Malachey finished lacing his boots and stood up, stamping a few times with his lame leg to get his foot properly settled. He put on his clean shirt, snapped the loops of his braces over his shoulders, crossed to the window and peered out, leaning over the table. His eyes took in the opposite Row, the closed, rain-glossed doors, the still, hooded windows, and beyond, dwarfing all, the massive grey bulk of the Mill. He saw how heavily the rain was falling, the myriad, driving streaks accentuated against the shadowy space between the edge of the roof slates of the cupped lengths of gutter pipe. His lips moved soundlessly with automatic aversion, and then he turned towards Neilly and Shemie, sitting on the old battered sofa slowly drawing on their boots.

'Here, you two, hurry yourselves up out o' that. And you, Neilly, get some bread cut. I could have had a regiment of boots on me, in the time you're sitting there.'

He swung a red-barred towel over his shoulders, tucked the edge under his shirt, and opened the flimsy hall door. The hall was dark and narrow, lighted only by a small pane of glass in the back door. Two buckets of water, with a black earthenware crock, stood on a form along the whitewashed wall. He took an enamel basin from a small stool at the end of the form and, pouring a few tinfuls of water into it, began to wash, stooping low over the basin, blowing noisily and splashing the water all over the stone tiles. He opened the back door and swooshed what was left into the yard. Then he limped back into the kitchen, drying himself vigorously, the breath rattling from his lips.

Neilly was pulling on his jersey, and Shemie was half-lying on the sofa engrossed in a pair of *Funny Wonder* comics. Malachey's face reddened with anger. He gave two quick hops, made a back-handed swipe at Shemie's ear, and, sweeping the comics into a ball, he flung them into the fire.

Shemie's eyes widened in bewilderment. Then he clapped a hand to his ear and burst into tears.

'Ah! What are you hitting me for?' he blubbered. 'I wasn't doing anything.'

'Hell and the devil commy-cut day be about you!' his father cried.

'Well I had on me, hadn't I?' Shemie wailed.

Malachey gripped his ear and hauled him onto his feet.

'Have you washed, have you?' he hissed. 'You're sitting there with the dirt ground into you, and your nose in Charlie Chaplin! Sweet God! But do I have to be always at your heels?' He pushed Shemie towards the hall door. 'Get down there, will you, out of my sight, and get yourself washed, before I do something I'll regret for the rest of my life.'

He swung round on Neilly, who was standing in the middle of the floor watching and listening with cringing fascination. Before he had time to juke, his father gave him a cuff as well.

'Go you, too, will you? You're stannin' there! I never seen such a pair of dirty clowns in all my life.'

Upstairs, Eugene tightened his lips and turned his eyes up to the ceiling.

'Every Sunday morning,' he muttered, every blinking Sunday morning.'

The latch lifted, and there entered hurriedly an old woman with a man's jacket gathered over her head and shoulders.

'God's truth,' she began, banging the door behind her. 'Eh? That's a morning and a half, eh?'

Malachey turned round from where he was standing, brushing his hair in front of the mirror over the fire-board. He saw that it was his mother, and turned back to the mirror without answering.

The old woman lowered the jacket and, shaking the raindrops from it, laid it on the counter and came through the red screen into the kitchen. She had on a man's old grey cap, which she seldom went without, either in the house or out, summer or winter.

'Has Kitty gone to Chapel?'

'Yes! She's away.'

The old woman tongue-clicked.

'Ha! She's a-laugh for running out on a morning like that. She'll get her end someday – Where're the students?'

Malachey lifted the kettle from the hook and set it on the hob, the boiling water japping from the spout and hissing on the hot iron.

'Aye! Where are they?'

Neilly and Shemie came clawing up the hall, eyes slitted and their necks craned to keep the water from trickling down under their shirts.

'Look at them, would you?' said their father, disgustedly. 'There's enough soap on them to wash an army.'

Their granny lifted the towel from the back of the armchair.

'Ah, let them alone, they're only childer yet.' She began to dry them, gouging the towel sharply into their soap-filled ears. 'Where's Eugene? Is he not up yet? What's happened now?' she asked, when she saw their red-rimmed eyes. 'Has there been another slaying match this morning again?'

Fresh tears squeezed from Shemie's eyes.

'He threw my good comics on the fire, so he did,' he sobbed, hiccupping gently, 'what I had to pay a penny for.'

'Mind who you're talking to now, boy,' his father cautioned, turning his head as he hung the heavy frying pan over the fire. 'Don't think you can come the tinman with me, just because your granny's here.'

'Ah, let them alone! You're too thick-witted with them altogether. You seem to forget that you were wrong yourself one day,' said his mother.

Malachey spread some bacon on the pan, adjusting the hook higher up the chimney. The bacon sputtered, and he licked his gravy-japped finger. He seemed somehow to be in a better humour now. His lips twisted with gentle irony.

'Ah, b'my soul, when I was like them, many's the wallup I got, and devil the bit of harm it done me. It's what the present generation is lost for.'

The old woman gave Shemie's shoulders a sudden rattle.

'You're a wee ottercrop anyway. You'd keep ten townlands going. Go and get your ties, the two of you, and come over with me out of the road, before somebody's split.'

Malachey made another wrestle with the hook, and looked around for something on which to clean his hands. The old woman handed him one of the boys' old shirts.

'Here, it'll have to be washed anyway – I didn't see any sign of Kelly's cart about this morning or last night. God knows where those two ligs have got to this time; away since Friday, and maybe lying in the back of some ditch somewhere.'

When she was angry and giving off, her head ticked slightly to and fro. Malachey nicked the bacon to prevent it curling; he did not say anything.

'What kind of an ould mad eegot is that Pachy fellow, anyway? He'd 'a' been better off if he'd 'a' stayed in Indi' in the army, instead of coming home here, to run wild through the country in a donkey and cart with screw-eyed Johnny Kelly. It's as good as a play.'

Neilly looked at his granny in puzzlement. It was strange to hear her speak like that about his uncle Pachy, and Johnny Kelly, when many's the time he had seen the two of them over in her house, drinking her aleplant, and sitting down to a tightener of potatoes and brown gravy, and everybody laughing and joking. Still, his granny was a strange sort of a woman; you could never tell when you had her. One minute she might be as great as anything with you; the next minute she's be biting your nose off.

Malachey shook some salt over the bacon.

'If Pachy wants to run about with Johnny Kelly, that's his own affair,' he said tonelessly. 'What's wrong with Kelly, anyway? There's worse than him going about.'

'Both of them'll be lifted yet, one of these fine days; that'll be the holy all of it. The police have had their eyes on that Kelly boyo long before Pachy came home. And Kitty's own brother, too, it's –'

She stopped suddenly as the front-door latch was lifted again, and a man poked his head round the corner of the partition. His blue eyes twinkled; he burst into a loud laugh, and, clapping his hands once together, he made a couple of hops round the counter, and whirled into a jig through the kitchen, his hands waving round his head. He was a big, broad man, with a fine mop of white hair and a long white moustache.

'Oh, what's the news! What's the news!
Baraney Grimly's pawned his shoes.
For to buy a new melodeon for the band.'

He halted breathlessly and thrust out his hand to the old woman. 'Hell to my soul, leave it there, Mrs Coyle. I haven't seen you in a month of Sundays. Right and well you're looking. How's yourself, Malachey?' He gave a couple more turns, the heavy gold watch chain over his waistcoat jingling. 'There you are,' he cried. 'Sixty-five in a loc of days and as supply' – a plocker of coughing seized him –

'Ha – ah-h-h – God bless us, o-ho – and as supple I'm saying, as I was thirty years ago.'

He looked down at Neilly and Shemie.

'How are you, my hardy men? Wait'll I see if I have any odd wing on me somewhere. Here!' He pressed a penny into each of the boys' hands. 'Don't get reckless now and spend it all at once.' He slapped a half-crown on the counter. 'Get us an ounce there, Malachey, God love you! My throat thinks I'm in the workhouse.'

Malachey limped down the hall to where he kept the tobacco, and the old woman remarked: 'You'll have to do on less, Mick, now that the Mill's going off again.'

'Ah, tut, woman, sense about you! The same old Mill will still be there, and going strong, when there's not a word about any of us.'

'Ah, I don't know, Mick,' sighed Malachey, handing over the Walnut. 'I'm afraid it's for the hatchet.'

'Ah, quit your worrying, man! Sure even if it does go off for a loc of weeks, it'll be open again in no time. Sure, didn't it go on again last year? Lord God, content yourself off a lovely morning like that.'

Neilly and Shemie burst out laughing.

'What are you laughing at, you wee midgets ye?'

'Come on,' said their granny, 'are you coming, you two? Tommy's just getting up.'

'Aye, away with you,' Mick shouted, 'and give your father's head peace.'

Malachey frowned.

'I thought I told you, Neilly, that you had to get the bread cut. Am I talking to the wall?'

'Och, away out of that,' his mother shot back. 'A child of his age cutting bread!' She gathered up her old jacket from the counter.

'They'll never be worth the nails to scratch theirselves with,' Malachey grunted, 'the way you have them.'

They all moved towards the door. Suddenly, Malachey turned

again from the bacon. From the knife in his hand, pale grease drops dripped onto the floor.

'You, Neilly! Did you throw your dirty water out?'

Neilly hesitated, frightened.

'No, Da.'

'Well, throw it out now, or damn the foot you'll set outside this door this morning!'

Neilly rushed down the hall. Old Mick, slapping his thighs, roaring with laughter and shouting goodbyes over his shoulder, lifted the latch and rushed out into the rain.

2

As Neilly, Shemie and their granny picked their steps as hastily as possible across the street, the Row was like a place of the dead. The only sound was that of the rustling of the rain and the harsh vomiting of the spouts. Not another sinner was to be seen. Every door was shut tight; the blistered paint and the rough, grey walls dark with the whippings of the rain.

The Row in which the Coyles' house stood was on a higher level than the other, which thus flooded more quickly, a regrettable fact acknowledged by the Mill owners, and accounting for the reduction in rent of the lower houses, which was only one and ninepence, sixpence less than that of those in the opposite side.

Already, as the Callan was rising, the dark floodwater was slowly swelling all along the gutter beneath the high cribben. They had to help their granny across the channel onto the footpath, and she burst into the house lamenting. Tommy, a dark-haired fellow of twenty-eight, was sitting on the stool at the fire, smoking a cigarette. He was wearing only his trousers; the upper part of his body was smooth, hairless, and glowing softly from the heat. Through the half-closed door of the small room came the crying of a child and the soft 'There now, there now' of a woman's voice.

An expression of annoyance flickered across the old woman's face.

'Tsk! Tsk! Has she the child up already!' She made to swing the old jacket from her shoulders, and took a quick step towards the room. Then, abruptly, she turned around and hoisted up the old coat again. 'My God the night!' she ejaculated. 'Do I have to go right back again?'

'What's wrong now?' Tommy asked. But the old woman swung the door open again and dashed out without answering. Through the window they peered out at her huddling once more across the fearsome street.

'A shocking women that, altogether,' Tommy sighed. 'What!'

'She has forgot the washing, I bet you, so she has,' Neilly said.

Though well over sixty, his granny was always on the go, a woman of tireless energy who, having wrought hard all her life, fretted now if she had not enough to keep her busy. She was always on the lookout for an extra job, and every Sunday morning she came over to her son's house to gather up any dirty washing that might be lying around, often wrestling with Kitty, if she happened to be there, for an extra shirt or sheet.

'What's wrong with the child, Tommy?' Shemie asked, moving towards the door. 'Will I go in?'

'No, don't go in, Shemie son,' Tommy said. 'Teasie will be lifting it in a minute.'

Neilly sat down at the table facing the window; Shemie crossed over to the fire, holding out his hands and screwing his face away from the heat. On each side of the fire the hob was piled up with damp turf and big, dark-yellow chips of fir.

'Is Eugene up yet?' Tommy inquired.

Shemie shook his head and backed away a few paces.

'My God! How do you stick that heat?'

Tommy hunched his shoulders over, rubbing his hands together.

'Ah, it's great, man dear. You don't know what you're missing. There! Here comes trouble, and we haven't a brick.'

The room door opened, and Teasie came out with the child. She sat down at the side of the fire, swaying the child gently to and fro. Her face and lips were pale, and her thick brown hair was clotted round her head. There was a strange, dreamlike air of detachment about her, a quality of resignation, or it could have been indifference, a deliberately cultivated trance-like indifference. Her eyes held a curiously remote expression, narrowed slightly as though she were thinking of something far away. The baby kept refusing the bottle, pushing it away with a damp, spidery hand, but the girl pointed it forward with calm, automatic patience, crooning softly and swaying her shoulders. She did not look at the child. Her eyes were fixed steadily on the window opposite, gazing unseeingly at the rain driving across the panes. Now and again she passed the tip of her tongue over her lips.

'What's the matter with the child, girl?' Tommy demanded. 'That would drive a man mad, listening to that.'

Teasie did not answer for a moment. Then, without taking her eyes from the window, she said, listlessly, and with a faint bitterness: 'If that's all you ever have to worry about, a child crying, you'll be a fortunate man indeed.'

Neilly and Shemie crowded round her, hands on their knees, gazing down at the child. They were both fascinated and repelled by its ugly, reddened, screwed-up face; the wet, toothless, bawling mouth.

'Maybe there's a pin sticking in it somewhere, Teasie,' Shemie suggested.

'No, it'll be all right in a minute, son,' Teasie said. 'Don't stand like that, like good boys, breathing into its wee face.'

She laid the unwanted milk bottle on the hob.

'Well, all right, darling, you're not hungry, you're not hungry. What's the matter then, love, eh? What's the matter? There now, ah, sure he's my own wee son.' She rose up and stood before the fire, staring vacantly at her reflection in the mirror over the fire-board, her shoulders still swaying rhythmically. 'There now! There now!'

The child's cries showed no sign of abating, and Tommy twisted a lock of his hair dementedly.

'Christ the night! This is a terror.' He twisted round on the stool. 'Any sign of your granny coming back yet, Shemie?'

Neilly glanced quickly over to the window. 'There she is!' he called. He rushed to the door, and ran out into the street, helping granny, once more, across the channel and into the house.

'That's the boy, Neilly, God love you,' she gasped, hanging up the old jacket behind the door. 'You're the only one who'll rise up off his lazy backside. Here, put that in the room for me.' She handed him a sheet-wrapped bundle of washing, and rushed angrily into the kitchen. 'That child's in convulsions,' she cried. 'What did you lift it for?'

'What do you think I lifted it for?' Teasie answered, almost inaudibly. 'If it would have lain on, you don't think I'd have lifted it.'

'Here! Give the child to me here, before it tears its wee lungs out.' She tried to wrest the child from Teasie's arms. 'A big hussy like you and you can't keep your own child quiet. How in under God you're going to get in your days is a mystery to me.'

Teasie turned the child away. 'Well, I'll have to learn sometime, won't I? Leave the child alone.'

'Teasie, don't be so cursed contrary,' Tommy said. 'If you can't pacify the child, hand it over to someone who can, before you land us all in the Asylum.'

Teasie looked down at him.

'Oh, yes!' she murmured bitterly. 'Your mother! I'm your wife, but am I ever in the right? Eh? Answer me that if you can. Will you?'

Tommy's face flushed angrily. He waved his hand.

'Ah! Sit down, sit down. You're talking there like a ha'penny book.'

Teasie let the old woman take the child. Lifting a cigarette from the fire-board, she lighted it and moved over to the window, pushing her hair up with her hand.

Whatever magic lay in the old woman's touch, the baby's wails began to subside the moment her arms went about it.

'Look at this milk! Tsk! Tsk! Tsk! It's stone cold.'

'The child's not hungry,' Teasie said shortly, without turning.

'The child's not hungry! Ah, of course the child's hungry. Would you put some hot water into a bowl till I warm this up a bit, or maybe that's too much to ask you?'

Teasie obeyed her silently. Then she returned to the window, standing with the backs of her thighs pressing against the edge of the table, her arms folded and her eyes narrowed against the thin cigarette smoke curving slowly past her expressionless face.

Neilly stood by the room door, straining his arms with pained embarrassment behind his back. He felt very sorry for Teasie, standing there like that. My granny, he thought, is too much of it sometimes. She is always fighting with her.

Tommy smiled over at him and stretched his arms forward luxuriously.

'Ah, that's a relief,' he sighed. 'Anything for a quiet life.'

Neilly opened the hall door and went down for a drink of water. As he tilted the cold rim of the tin to his lips, he heard Shemie calling excitedly: 'Hi! Oh, Neilly, look! Tommy can stick his hands right down into the fire!'

Neilly wiped his lips and came back into the kitchen. He stretched his hand tentatively towards the fire.

'Ah, sure, anybody at all can do that,' he said.

Shemie gave his arm a push.

'Put it right in. That's no good.'

Neilly yelped; the heat searing his fingers. Shemie crushed in against Tommy as his brother made a swipe at him.

'You wee skitter ye.'

Tommy crouched over the younger boy.

'If you hit him now, Neilly, I'll warm your ear,' he warned, half laughing.

'I got a belt in the ear off my father this morning over the head of him,' Neilly shouted. 'Never mind, I'll get you again. Just wait.' He blew tenderly on his fingers, pursing up his lips in an affected grimace of pain.

'Why, was there another fight this morning again?' Tommy asked.

'Fight be damned,' the old woman snarled, shuffling her feet fiercely. 'If you two don't sit quiet and behave yourselves, out you'll go on the palms of your neck, never to return. You, Shemie! You're the greatest little torment I ever seen. It would have been a charity if your father had flung you into the fire after your comics.'

Depressed by this reminder of his comics' sad fate, Shemie gazed woefully into the fire.

'He'll have to pay for them, so he will,' he muttered.

'Tommy, are you going out to the bullets after dinner?' Neilly asked. 'I'm going.'

Tommy crawled even closer to the fire.

'Tut, man! Sense about you. In that rain?'

'I bet you a pound it'll be over by ten o'clock. Are you game? Teasie, are you going? How does it come that girls never go to the bullets? It's always only men you see there.'

'Indeed I couldn't tell you, son,' Teasie said tonelessly. 'I suppose it's because it's only for men.'

The old woman lifted the child's bottle from out of the hot water and dried it on the hem of her apron. She drew at the milk to test it, and then offered it to the child. The child's tiny hands clutched at it, and it began to suck greedily, uttering little bubbling groans, while the old woman tenderly wiped at the dribbles of milk which, in the child's eagerness, kept spilling from the corners of its mouth. She looked up.

'Neilly, your father sent your ties over. Look in that old jacket behind the door. Tommy, take those ties and put them on for them, will you? And rouse yourself up out of that and get yourself shaved. A nice-looking ornament you are, I must say, sitting there in your figure.'

Tommy took the ties lazily.

'Ah, hould your tongue, woman dear. Oceans of time yet.' He wriggled his broad white shoulders. 'Teasie, run and see if the front door's closed, like a good girl, before I'm frozen to death.'

'Hell to your soul, didn't I close it after me?' his mother cried. 'I never seen such a coulrifed craythur in all my life.'

Tommy winked at the two boys.

'As true as God this is the draughtiest house I ever seen. I'm not kidding you, but I seen me sitting in front of this fire here, my chest a-roasting and the coat-tails flying up over my head. Teasie, throw a taste of coal on there, God love you, and make yourself generally useful.'

Teasie hesitated, looked up at him for a moment with compressed lips. Then she went down the hall to the coal-hole and returned with a shovelful of coal, which she hitched onto the fire. A dense cloud of smoke and sparks rushed up the chimney, followed in a second by a fresh burst of flame.

Tommy reached up and patted her on the back.

'Ah! Ah! But she's a great girl. I wouldn't swap my Teasie for – Don't go away now, pidge, and as soon as I get on me I'll give you a great big birdie all to yourself.' He turned back to the fire. 'God bless us, but that's lovely.'

'If God hasn't said it, you'll be roasted there some day yet,' his mother said. Her eyes swept over the window. 'Tsk! Tsk! Did you ever see such a morning. We're in for the quare flooding match of it again, I'm thinking. When you're at Chapel this morning,' she ordered Neilly and Shemie in a half-jeering voice, 'say a couple of prayers for the rain to go over. You're the prayingest connection I ever came across.'

The child finished its milk, and the old woman put him back in the pram.

'Are you going to get yourself ready, girl?' she said to Teasie. 'It's almost nine o'clock, if you want to be in time for ten. You needn't be waiting for that rain to go over.'

'Who's going to wash the child when it gets up?' Teasie asked.

'Ah, get on you, and away you go. I'll do that. Washing a child's not the rent of the town.'

Teasie came over to the fire-board slowly and lifted a comb from it.

'That's the girl, Teasie,' Tommy said, looking up at her. 'You get ready and –' he rose and leant towards her, pursing his lips up and making a sweet, cheeping sound – 'there's one birdie for you, and if you behave yourself and wash your ears well, I'll consider your case for another. Or would you rather have it now?'

Teasie turned her head away.

'Don't act the cod, Tom. I'm trying to comb my hair.'

Neilly and Shemie began to laugh as they saw a faint smile struggling through her clouded eyes. Tommy put his arms around her neck.

'Ah now, Teasie! I know you like the bird-birds –'

The old woman came up the hall with a brush.

'Shift yourself out of that, you ould mad eejit and get on you. Look at the time it is!' She knocked the brush up against his ankles, laughing, and he trailed his semmit off the line across the fireplace.

'Wait, wait, give us a chance. I'm not armed.'

'I wouldn't mind, only it takes you an hour shaving. I don't know why you can't shave in the room like a Christian, or in the glass there above the fire-board. I never can get a hand's turn done when you commandeer that table.'

A long time before Tommy had a lot of pimples on his face, and had to shave at the table, where there was plenty of light, so as to avoid cutting himself. Now, even after eight or nine years, the habit still remained.

'Why don't you shave at night, Tommy, like my father?' Shemie suggested. 'Then you wouldn't have to shave in the morning.'

Tommy came out of the room carrying a stand with a small, framed mirror. He sat it on the table, before the window, and peered into it, scraping his hand over his shadowed cheeks.

'D'ye hear that?'

The boys backed away in alarm.

'Granny, he's going to give us a bear's rub.'

The old woman was sweeping the floor. The tiles were covered with sheets of newspaper, which she had to hold down with her feet as she ran the brush over them.

'Och, Tommy! Quit the play-acting now and leave them alone. You'll have the child up next.' She looked up suddenly. 'Here, there's your mother back, you two! Away you go, and good riddance.'

Glancing quickly out through the window, the boys saw their mother stop outside their door, opposite, and nod farewell to an older woman in a shawl. Shouting 'So long's, they rushed out, slapping the door roughly behind them, while the old woman rattled the brush and barged angrily at them through the rain-distorted panes.

3

Half past one!

The rain was easing up. In the gloomy heavens, little patches of clear blue appeared, islands in a glowering sea of cloud.

A crowd had gathered at the Bridge round the Corner, and more were arriving every minute, coming in little groups from both directions; down the Asylum Hill from town, and up the Loughall Road. They sauntered about, smoking and talking excitedly. Some stood leaning against the rough Asylum wall; others craned over the stone parapet of the Bridge, gazing at the thick brown flood water coiling from under the arches, and the white flower of their spits being swept away out of sight, or being sucked down amid the numerous eddies and whorls.

A couple of fellows where throwing practice shots up and down the road, the bullet, a round iron ball of 1¾ pounds, bucking and hammering over the wet surface. A young fair-haired fellow was standing against the Asylum wall, chatting with Malachey and a few other men. Once, when the bullet curved towards him, he kepped it with his foot and took a walk back for a shot. This was Macklin, one of the most celebrated names in bullet-throwing circles. A year before, Macklin was practically an unknown, but now he had blossomed into a brilliant thrower, winning match after match and inspiring his followers with such confidence that they had begun negotiating for a great match with the Hammer-man himself. Macklin, however, was not throwing today.

Just before two o'clock, Neilly and Shemie came racing round the Corner, kicking up their heels with joy. Their mother, on seeing the tints of sunlight, had at last given into their pleadings.

'All right, put your coats on,' she cried, 'But remember, if you get even as much as a thimbleful of rain on them you needn't come back the night more.'

They writhed up the Bridge wall, crying out at the height of the river and at the gleaming sheet of water over in Sherry's field, where the river had swelled over the bank. At the sight, Neilly felt almost sorry that the rain had gone over. If there had been a flood, maybe he would not have had to go to school in the morning . . .

During the betting there was a great hum of voices. Boys, playing tig, ran in and out among the gesticulating groups, and mongrels cringed about, letting out a yelp now and again as they got into someone's way and received an automatic boot in the ribs. Disturbed by the noise, rooks from the high, bare trees, beyond the Asylum wall, circled about, cawing harshly.

'Mister! Will I mind your bike, mister?'

Neilly and a few of his pals crushed through the crowd, hopefully offering their services. This, indeed, was Neilly's major interest in bullet matches, the chance of getting a bicycle to look after, so that in the wage of the score, and safely hidden from the owner's eye, he could practice to his heart's content; sometimes heeling into the nettles in the ditches, or going on his mouth and nose over the handlebars, with a sickening but rarely disheartening regularity.

When the betting finished, the crowd became greatly animated, the men clearing their throats, shrugging their shoulders, clapping their hands together and shouting to the youngsters to get away home out of it, if they didn't want their legs broken.

At that moment, a horrible yell, as of someone in mortal agony, came from over and beyond the high Asylum wall.

'Half past two,' the men called. 'Right! Let's get the score started!'

This scream was heard every day, year in and year out, at exactly half past two. No one seemed to know the reason behind it for sure, or from what unfortunate throat it issued. It was said that it came from a man who had been bitten by a mad dog one day after half past two, and upon each day, at the fateful moment, he gave vent to his berserk howl.

Daly, the first thrower, walked back for a long run. Some wits began to shout: 'So long, Paddy!' after him. Then he turned about twenty yards away, jigging the bullet up and down in his hand, taking in the lie of the road, and the crouching figure of his marker, a hundred yards down. He ran up on the tips of his toes, increasing his speed gradually until, as he came up to the grass butt, he was going all out. He leapt into the air, his head falling limply back, and the bullet hit the road like a shot out of a gun. It drummed down the centre with frightening speed, and flashed through the marker's straddled legs without his having to alter his position an inch. Then it cut in towards the footpath on the right-hand side, along the Asylum wall, smacked off the high cribben and slanted back across the road away down past the Stony Loaning. It thudded against the bank and bumped off again on down the road. Then, falling back gradually into the sheugh, it spun along for a few more yards and stopped. A great shout went up. It was a magnificent first shot of over two hundred yards. Slaps were rained on Daly's shoulder as he donned his jacket, while a tussock of grass was flung down to mark his shot.

His opponent, Toner, took a much shorter run, but there was immense power behind his bullet as it went battering along. There was a twist on it, however, and before it reached the marker it could be seen curving in towards the high grassy bank on the left. A low 'Ah-h-h-h!' went up from the crowd, and the marker walked across the road waving his hands above his head. Then there came a great shout as the bullet, smacking against a large stone in the sheugh, leapt once again into the centre of the road, slashing with such force through a deep puddle that two gleaming wings of water swung high up on either side. The bullet stayed in the centre of the road, but its power was waning. Finally it came to a halt a few yards behind Daly's mark. Toner took his coat amid murmurs of sympathy and praise. 'Never mind, Joe, a grand shot still and all. Keep it up and the score's yours.'

Neilly and a few other boys had been successful in their hunt for bicycles. They followed shakily behind the crowd, Neilly riding torturously through the frame, a look of agonised concentration on his face. His right leg, at each revolution, squirmed away from the chain to keep the oil from his stockings. Now and then shouts, and bursts of cheering, reached them from the forefront of the score, but the sights which inspired them had no interest for the boys. All their attention was riveted on the task of learning how to ride a bicycle . . .

One mile out, the distant reverberation of thunder drew upwards the eye of the crowd. For the first time they became aware of the terrible sky stretching above them. The vivid blue patches had long since vanished, leaving a desolate immensity like a vast sheet of lead riveted over the world. A deathly hush pervaded everything. Nothing moved, with the exception of two crows beating hurriedly away out over the lonely, dimming fields.

Daly, in his shirt sleeves and about to throw, hesitated uneasily. Then the crowd came back to reality.

'Come on, man; come on, throw your shot. We haven't got all night.'

Daly cleared his throat, walked back quickly, and then commenced his run towards his mark, changing his direction a few feet off, and legging it into the ditch, as, with a suddenness, frightening in spite of its imminence, it began to rain again. The drops came down in a solid silver sheet, bitter, swirling, drenching rain that crushed hissing on the road, instantly soaking almost to the skin every man in the score. Like animals they scuttled for shelter, thrusting deep into the hedges on either side of the road, heedless of the thorns and briars, coats drawn like capes over their shoulders. A few ran towards McGill's gate, wrestling frantically with the bolt, and sprinting up the little rocky loaning under the railway bridge.

Neilly and his companions had joined the rest in that first dash for shelter, flinging their bicycles roughly into the sheugh. The hedges, gutted by winter, offered little protection, and the boys crushed further and further back, panting and wincing as the thorns drove into their hands and legs. Neilly felt the rain stabbing at the top of his head, and onto his bare knees. It streamed around his cheeks and down his neck; a large drop hung glistening from his nose, forming again each time it blew off. No matter how he twisted and turned, he could find no shelter. Clatter after clatter of thunder broke across the fields.

A coldness closed around Neilly's heart as he saw the lightening tickle with silent menace down the sky. A little half-hysterical giggle broke from his lips, and one of the other boys began to whimper with fear.

'Oh mother, it's the end of the world. Please take me home. Oh please take me home!'

Suddenly there was a loud cry from up the road. Peeping out, Neilly saw young Shemie running up and down, shouting his name dementedly: 'Neilly, Neilly! Ah, Neilly!' the name blurring into a scream of terror. Neilly sprang out and then, fifty or sixty yards up, he saw another figurine, that of Eugene, lunge out onto the road after Shemie, and haul him back under the hedge.

Neilly sprinted up and crushed in with them.

Eugene had Shemie clasped to his breast, and was petting him gently.

'There now, it's all right Shemie. Look, here's Neilly now. Don't be crying, like a good boy. Sure an old drop of rain wouldn't do you any harm.'

'What's wrong with him, Eugene?' Neilly cried. 'I thought he was with you.'

'He came running up the road there,' one of the fellows crushed in beside him said. 'The thunder's scared him. He must have got stuck in with a crowd he didn't know.' He offered the young boy a penny. 'Look Shemie, here's and odd wing for you here. Don't be crying now, man dear, sure you're as sound as a row of houses.'

Neilly closed his hand round the back of his young brother's knee and gradually Shemie's sobs subsided.

The rain had lightened a little from its first fierce avalanche, but it still fell torrentially, sweeping in bitter guts up the road and across the misty fields. From nearby came the hollow drumming of the swollen sheugh water, as it raced into a grating. Now and then a figure broke from the hedge towards McGill's gate, pelting madly for the shelter of the railway bridge.

'Here,' said Eugene, 'I'm going to make a dash for it too. Who's game? Neilly, you take Shemie's other hand. Are you right?'

A little cluster of them broke from the hedge, but they had only gone a few steps when Neilly hesitated, nearly dragging his brothers to a halt.

'The bike,' he cried. 'A fellow gave me his bike to look after.'

Eugene's streaming face twisted with fury.

'Leave it there!' he screamed. 'Come on, will you?'

But Neilly had dropped Shemie's hand, and was legging it back down the road.

The other boys were still huddled abjectly into the hedge.

'Come on! Come on!' Neilly yelled. 'Make for the Bridge.' He grabbed at his machine, and after a moment of hesitation the others followed, pushing desperately off the road, lunging against the gate and swerving madly through the cart ruts in the loaning, the crowd beneath the Bridge cheering ironically.

'I've a good mind to warm your lug for you, boy,' Eugene said, as Neilly set the bicycle against the wall of the Bridge.

'What d'ye think you're on?'

A man in a soft hat pushed forward.

'Here! You're the hardy man I left my ould gate with, aren't you? Well, there's a tanner for taking your work so seriously.'

A shout of laughter went up and Neilly gaped in astonishment. In the entire history of his bullet-following experience, this was without precedent. He saw his father and Tommy smile over at him, and confused with joy and embarrassment, he turned his head away, reddening deeply.

Time passed. The rain showed not the slightest sign of easing up. To make matters worse, great flurries of it kept blowing in at both sides of the Bridge, forcing the crowd to step back uneasily through the clammy, cowclap of the ground.

'This cursed Bridge will be down on the top of us any minute,' someone prophesied, as a terrible peal of thunder burst out directly above.

Shemie gave a scream and ran from Eugene to his father, and could hardly be pacified.

'Christ the night, this is fearful,' Malachey muttered. 'There now! Look, you're wringing. Tsk! Tsk! Your mother will go stone mad.'

Fellows still came running up from the road, but the space beneath the Bridge would not hold them all.

'Ah, to hell with it!' Tommy cried. 'Are you coming, Malachey?'

He had been thinking that, as there was sure to be a flood now, and with his house on the bad side he would have to get up quickly and give his mother and Teasie a hand.

Malachey shook his head.

'No. Away you on, Tommy, and see to the ould doll. We'll have to square up about the match first. Shemie, you better go home with your uncle Tommy. Your mother will be up the walls.' But Shemie only clung more tightly. Tommy waited no longer.

'Well, you fix it up any way you like. I'll tell Kitty you'll be home directly.'

He, and a few other fellows from the Row, bolted off, their shoes ringing against the stones in the lane.

'Well,' sighed Malachey, 'there'll be no more bullets the day, boys; we might as well go home as best as we can. This rain's on for amen.'

They began handing back the bets, Macklin reading the names from the notebook and Malachey handing out the money. They had nearly finished when, suddenly, they were startled by a loud shout from down by the gate. Looking up, they saw a fellow standing at the bottom of the loaning waving his hand; behind him, and half hidden by the hedge, was a donkey and cart.

The stranger gave the gate a push, and came walking up without haste, as if it were a day in the depth of summer. He wore an old cap and an old, ragged showerproofed coat.

'It's Pachy,' Malachey murmured in amazement.

Pachy came up with a little mocking smile at the stir he was causing; a dark, hardy-looking fellow of about twenty-six. He moved with a slow, graceful swagger unconcealed by his rough clothes, and contrasting strangely with them.

'Well, well, well,' he said, 'by the left!' looking over the faces before him. 'There's wiser men in the Asylum. Imagine picking a day like that to stand under a railway bridge! What happened the score? Don't tell me that you let a little taste of rain like that break it up? Why didn't you postpone it? I would have held the bets for you.'

'What brought you down here?' Malachey laughed. 'We thought you were miles away? Where's Kelly?'

'Look! If you don't get out quick from in under that Bridge, it'll be the priest and not Kelly you'll be asking for. And Neilly and Shemie here too. My God the night!'

'I'm here too, Pachy,' Eugene cried, poking his hand up.

'What? Here, come on, juldee! Kate'll be astray in the mind.'

'Wait, Pachy,' Malachey said. 'How many more names, Jim?'

'Well, that's all here. There's six or seven went earlier.'

'Come on, then. I can see them again sometime.'

The men pulled their coats around them, peering out fearfully across the shrouded fields, their hearts failing at the thought of the jostling match before them. A few sighs of resignation – 'Ah, well there's nothing else for it' – and then, the anguished scramble back down through the gate.

4

The little donkey clopped gamely along, the wheels of the cart crunching over the fine, sodden gravel at the side of the road. A group of boys jogged behind, holding on, with Pachy turning and shouting: 'I can't take you, we're overloaded as it is. This donkey's jossed.' But the boys trailed doggedly on, Neilly and Shemie sat huddled up, grinning back at them.

Pachy turned again to Malachey.

'Yes, we met Tommy at the Corner, and he told us where you were, so I just took a run on down.' He cocked an eye upwards. 'That sky looked wicked. We're in for the grandfather of all floods the night.'

'Where's your man, then?' Malachey asked.

'Who? Oh, Kelly? I left him at the Corner to mind the donkeys.'

'What donkeys?'

'Our donkeys,' Pachy replied, deliberately laconic.

Neilly turned round interestedly.

'Have you got some more donkeys, Pachy? How many?'

'Ask no questions and you'll be told no lies, as the fellow once said to the policeman.'

Malachey gave a chuckle, half amusement, half expasperation.

'You're as mad as a hatter, you and that Kelly fellow. Where have you been all this time?'

'Just having a jaunt around for the good of our health. We got the donkeys chape down at the Moy fair. They're a bit on the bony side, but they'll draw in a few extra ha'pence when we get them fattened up a bit. Keep a tight grip on them bags there, you boys ye.'

Pachy directed Neilly and Shemie, as he waved his hand at some of the panting men they were beginning to pass. 'Put an inch to your step there, Eugene, man dear, a young fellow like you. I thought you said you'd be up long before us.'

Eugene waved back wordlessly, his face bright with exertion and rain.

'Potatoes,' said Malachey, 'eh? Whereabouts did you pick them up?'

'Well, Malachey, I'm surprised at you asking that. There's only one place I know of where you can pick potatoes up – in a field.'

'You can get potatoes in a shop, Pachy,' Shemie offered eagerly, proud of being able to contribute to the conversation.

Pachy inclined his head solemnly, the quirk of irony and mockery deepening on his lips.

'Yes, he's right, the boy's absolutely right! You can get potatoes in a shop. But you see, Shemie boy, the way of it is with me, somehow or another I never have liked dealing in a shop. For some strange reason, the people there have got a very bad habit. If you want anything, you have to graze their hand first – get up there, Jimmy, or whatever your name is, or we'll not get home the night,' – he sighed – 'Yes, it's very strange. I can't understand it.'

Shemie looked at him in puzzlement. Malachey let out his grim little chuckle again.

'You'll wonder where you spent your summer, boy, one of these days, if you find yourself wakening up to a breakfast of bread and water.'

They were rattling past the Asylum wall now. Through the darkening air the Corner of the Row was in sight.

'Where're the donkeys, Pachy?' Shemie asked, straining his eyes. 'I can't see any.'

'Never mind, they're about somewhere. Ah, well, home, sweet home, and the fire out! Hold on tight, boys.'

They turned into the Row, Neilly and Shemie laughing wildly as the cart gave a great lurch, almost flinging them off. In excitement and wonder they looked down the Row.

A sheet of water stretched from the low side halfway across the street, from the bottom almost up to the Corner. All the lower windows on the flooded side were dark, the occupants having retreated upstairs from the flooded kitchens. Through the top windows, the yellow gaslight streamed down onto the cold, rain-freckled water. On the other side, most of the upstairs windows were lit as well as the bottom, as the people prepared for their evacuation also. Through the top windows children waved and made faces at each other, their high-pitched chatter echoing piercingly along the street. Here and there, on the side which the water had not yet reached, women craned over the half-doors seeing, in their imagination, the dark waters swirling and edging through their neighbours' houses, and judging fearfully every inch of its sinister and inexorable approach to their own.

The relfection of the gaslight rippled like silk as the cart cut through the edge of the flood; Pachy waved his hand in answer to the greetings that were shouted at them; Neilly and Shemie peering down between their legs, at the water wriggling round the wheel, and shouting out as, down at the bottom, they glimpsed the four donkeys huddled miserably in the corner.

Kitty, at the rattle of the cart, had rushed to the door. She stood peering out with angry impatience as they approached – a woman with a head of auburn hair, still rich and thick, though tinged here and there with grey, and a pale, sharp, rather pinched face which belied the wiry vigour of her slight, work-thinned body.

'My God, this holy day and hour!' she cried, as the cart stopped outside the door. 'A nice-looking set of ornaments you are, I must say, sitting there like pilgrims in the night, and the water running out of you. Where did you leave that Eugene fellow?'

'Ah, the bold Kate, there,' Pachy greeted. 'How's the heart? I can't stay. I've got to see to my dearly beloved brethren down there at the dunkill. Where's Kelly? Have you seen him?'

'I'm sure you're uneasy about my heart. That same fellow, roaming mad through the country as if nobody owned you. Come in, come in, for God's sake, before the whole Row is out.'

She slapped the door behind them.

'You might have sent the childer home, Malachey, at least, standing under a railway bridge off a day like that, and the wind whistling through them.'

'Ah, now, don't start, for God's sake! Let's get into the house first. You'd think I was a weather expert to hear you.'

With Kitty reading them out fiercely, they all crushed round the counter, pulling up at the sight of a man sitting in the armchair by the fire in his shirtsleeves, with a large mug of tea in his hand and a plate of bread and jam balanced on his knee. He set his plate and mug on the hob and rose up smiling. He was a fellow of about thirty, with a lean, bony face and a little turn in his eye. He had a strange habit, no matter where he was or what he was doing, of glancing up and looking quickly around him as though someone had suddenly and unexpectedly called his name.

'How're ye, Malachey?' he greeted. 'Wild class of day that.'

'Hello, Johnny! Dambut is it yourself?'

'Sit down, Johnny,' Kitty told him, 'don't disturb yourself on their accounts. Sit down and finish your tea.'

'Well, well, well, by the left!' said Pachy, coming over to the fire and stretching his hands out. 'God help the donkeys anybody leaves you to look after. Changed and all too!' He looked at his friend's dry clothes, and the old wet garments draped steaming over an upended stool.

'Kitty here called me down from the Corner,' Kelly said, taking a drink of tea, his thumb hooked around the spoon in the mug. 'Are the donkeys all right out there?'

'Well, Christ the night! It wouldn't have ate you to have taken them in with you. Kate wouldn't have minded sure. What do you say, Malachey? Dambut after all, the poor ould donkeys deserve a bit of a hate too. That's a class fire.'

'Come on, come on!' Kitty was crying, wrenching the coats off Neilly and Shemie. 'Get those wet things off for the love and honour of God. I told you not to go out. I could look over it if I hadn't warned you. But no! Well, if I'm lying and spared, I'll see that's the last bullet match you'll ever set your heels after. You'll sit in the house like other childer.' She ran her hands distractedly over the boys' shoulders. 'Soaking! Soaking! If I haven't the times of it amongst you. I'm cleaning and drying from I get up in the morning till I go to bed at night.' She gave Shemie's shoulder a rattle. 'And you. If it's not one thing it's another. If you're not falling into the River Callan, you're coming home drownded with the rain. Lord God, Malachey, I thought you had more sense. Where am I going to find room to dry all these clothes?'

'Ah, take it easy, woman dear,' Pachy soothed. 'Don't get you be'rd in a blaze. Here! In the name of the wee man sure you wouldn't call that wet now! Stand well up to the fire, you boys ye, while you have the chance, before your mother brings the donkeys in, and you'll be as dry as a bone in a minute.'

'Oh, you're a great fellow,' Kitty answered bitterly. 'You'll do a lot. You're a great fellow indeed! Here you two, strip off you there, every stitch. I'll put the bullets out of your head. Come on, come on, before I lose my patience altogether. Johnny Kelly won't take a bite out of you, I'm sure.'

'Ah, for God's sake, give our heads peace and let them alone,' cried Malachey, trailing his shirt over his head. 'A drop of rain won't kill them.'

Kitty took a dry shirt, socks and semmit from the line across the fire and threw them on the sofa beside him.

'Well, I hope so. But you needn't worry. It isn't you who has the bother of looking after them when they're laid up. And I hope we won't hear you barking the morrow or the next day yourself.'

'You never heard me barking in the reign of your puff –' At that moment the front-door latch clicked.

'Here's Eugene now,' cried Kitty, turning round. 'Where in the name of – oh, it's yourself, Mrs Sheridan.'

'Hell's curse,' gasped Malachey, gathering up his shirt and semmit and hopping, half naked, through the room door, with Pachy and Kelly rocking with laughter after him.

'I thought you were Eugene, Mrs Sheridan. My mind's distracted. These ones are only after coming in on the top of me like drownded rats.'

An old crowled-up woman, with a coat pulled round her, sidled up to the counter.

'Ah, daughter dear, isn't it a terror? What's to become of us at all, at all. Give us a box of matches, like a decent girl, God love you, and a couple of candles. May God and His blessed and holy Mother look down upon us this night. Is that yourself, Pachy, and Johnny Kelly there? It's as long as I mind since I seen you. Are you bravely?'

'Get out from in under my feet, will you?' Kitty cried, as Neilly and Shemie, completely naked, tried to hide behind her.

'Ah, don't be afraid of me, childer dear. Run up to the fire and warm yourselves.'

'Pachy! Pachy! Throw us in those dry trousers, will you, before I'm froze to death?' Malachey hissed from the room. 'No! No, not those! Yes, that's them! Good!'

Receiving her purchases, the old woman was turning to go when once again the door swung open. Eugene plattered in, gasping and red in the face.

'Phew! Old Eoin McCluskey collapsed on the road, and we

had to carry him home. Oh, hello, Mrs Sheridan – That's a terrible evening. Mind that big puddle there up at Toner's door. It would take you over the head if you went into it. Phe-ew, what a night!'

Murmuring ejaculations and blessings, the old woman stumbled out.

Malachey came out into the kitchen screwing his shoulders through his braces.

'He had to make a rush for it.' Pachy laughed. 'Old Mrs Sheridan caught him in his figure.'

'She caught us too, Eugene,' Shemie shouted. Neilly bent over and put his hand on his hip.

'Childer dear,' he croaked, 'run up to the fire and warm your wee selves.'

Amid the laughter, his mother gave him a soft cuff in the ear. 'That'll do you, acting the big fellow there!'

'You hurry yourself up, boy, and get those wet clothes off,' his mother ordered Eugene. 'What are you going to do?' she snapped at Pachy. 'Are you going to catch yourself on, and change into these old things that Johnny Kelly brought over, before you catch a plocker that you'll carry to the grave?'

'What about the donkeys, my God! If you're not going to take them in, I'll have to bring them down to our field. I can't leave them out there all night.'

'Our field?' Kitty repeated sarcastically. 'Our field? Where's that, will you tell me?'

Pachy would not provoke.

'Well, Horanses field then.'

'H'm, they'll soon get shot out of there! Just because a man lets you keep one ould donkey in his field, doesn't mean to say that he's going to put with a regiment of them.'

'Come on, Pachy,' Eugene offered, 'I'll give you a hand down with them.'

'Aha! Well dare you set your foot outside this door the night more! He's big and ugly enough to look after his own donkeys.'

'No, Eugene, you stay here and take off those wet clothes,' Pachy said, amiably. 'What would take you out there again, and Kelly sitting there with his belly full of bread and jam?'

'Ah, you wouldn't bring Johnny out again, and him changed and all? I'll be all right, Mother. I can't possibly get any wetter. It won't take us long.'

'Oh, I'm tired arguing,' Kitty said wearily, arranging the wet clothes as best she could on the line and on chairs around the fire. 'No, Johnny, you're not in the way. Sit where you are. I'll never get these dried, never.'

As Pachy and Eugene moved towards the door, Pachy added carelessly: 'Oh, Kate, I was nearly forgetting there. We brought a couple o' stone of potatoes down. It's handy having a roughness of them about.'

They came struggling in with the lumpy, sodden bagful, and without speaking, Kitty opened the hall door for them. They went back to the cart, and Eugene returned with the bag of cabbages, followed by Pachy with three hens.

'These blinking roosters,' he said, 'will not keep off the road. They came running right in under the wheels of the cart. You can't avoid them.'

The long wrung necks dangled limply, and the feathers were dirty and bedraggled. He held up the birds critically.

'Oh, look, boys.' Neilly and Shemie crowded round open-mouthed. 'Where'd you get them from, Pachy? I didn't see them on the cart.' Shemie stretched his hand out tentatively. 'Are they dead, Pachy, are they?'

The heads swung up suddenly, and the boys recoiled.

'Are they bejapers, dead! You mind out. They have it in for you, for sitting on them under the oilsheet.'

'They must have got caught in the spokes,' Malachey commented, in the same ironical tone. 'Their necks are brave and well stretched.'

'I'm telling you, it'd take you to have a dozen pair of eyes on the road these days. We were nearly over a young pig twice or three times. Kelly here is a wild man at the reins. Where'll I put them, Kate?'

Kitty sighed resignedly.

'Ah, I can see it's only a waste of time talking to you, Pachy,' she said, the hardness leaving her voice for the first time since he came in. 'Hang them up behind the back door. I can see visions of us all winding up in Crumlin Jail one of these days. That'll be the end of it yet.'

Pachy laughed.

'You're right, Kate. That'll be the final resting place of us all. There's one for the old woman there,' he called from down the hall, 'and a loc of potatoes. But she'll have to wait, we can't bring them over now.' He came back into the kitchen. 'She's like yourself, Kate, that old woman; she would fight with her own toenails, but many a good tightener she gave Kelly and me just the same.'

5

In the rain-pierced gaslight, Kitty watched the cart jolting and sloshing up the street, the four donkeys trailing behind. It turned the Corner, and the rattle of the wheels hardened and dimmed over the firmer, smoother surface of the road.

Kitty elbowed the boys down off the half-door.

'Come on, in you get, they're away.' The boys were dressed only in their shirts. 'Here! What do you think you're on, hanging over the door like that? You two'll get what's coming to you, if you're not very careful.'

The boys hopped down giggling, and ran back round to the fire.

Kitty came in, shrugging her shoulders and rubbing her elbows.

'Ah-oh! There's a stepmother's breath out there. That water's nearly up to the cribben, Malachey. I think it's time we started shifting a few things. You and your donkeys, Kelly,' she joked. 'Hell will never be full till you're in it. Here, you two, hurry up and get something on, and get off up the stairs out of this. It's always the same when there's anybody in. Give you an inch and you take a span.'

'Ah, Mammy,' Shemie wailed, 'it's too early for bed yet awhile. Look! The wee hand's at six and the big hand's at two. It's only two o'clock.'

'Ah, get away,' Neilly sneered. 'He can't even read the clock yet.'

'It's ten past six, Shemie,' Kelly instructed. 'You weren't far wrong.'

Shemie frowned up at the clock.

'Where does the ten come in?'

'Come on,' cried Kitty, 'plenty of time for arithmetic after. You needn't go to bed yet, though you won't be very long out of it. There is a fire in the front room and the gas is lit and all; take yourselves off now and let me get my head shired. I'll cut you a piece of bread for the time being. There's no use in making the tea yet a wee while, till we get everything upstairs and the other two stud ends are back. The flood'll be in on us in a minute.'

The boys took their cuts of bread and made for the stairs, their feet slapping on the bare tiles.

'And don't let me hear any pulling and hauling going on up there,' Kitty cried after them. 'I'll be up myself shortly.'

Malachey rose and, going to the door, opened it and peered out into the street. A flurry of rain swung in against his face, and he slapped the door again hurriedly.

'God the night! That's wicked.'

'Bad, Malachey?' Kelly asked.

'Bad, aye! It's not taking time to be bad. Give us a hand with these few cases of minerals, Johnny, will you? What about coal, Kitty? Is there enough upstairs?'

'Well, I left a few bucketfuls up. There's nothing else to hold it in. We'll just have to use the oil stove when it's gone.'

Malachey and Johnny came backing out of the room with a large case of minerals, and set it gently on the old sofa. On the top of that they piled two more, the bottles knocking against their wooden slots.

'Well, it's a bit lopsided,' Malachey remarked, 'but there's nowhere else to put them.'

Kitty hooked some shoes and slippers out from under the sofa, and pushed them between the necks of the bottles.

Next they opened the drawer beneath the counter and transferred all its contents onto the table – bags of flour, baking powder, washing soda, soap, salt, and a few other commodities. Out of another chest of drawers in the room Malachey and Johnny wrenched the two bottom drawers, containing clothes, and left them on the counter, while down the hall Kitty rummaged about, trying to find someplace to put the pots and pans and other odds and ends lying in under the form, against the wall. One or two other jobs; the packing of a few empty biscuit tins with some vital necessities, tea, sugar, bread, butter and so on, completed the most of their preparations, and Kitty struggled up the stairs with an armful of damp shirts and trousers.

'The coats will have to stay down here,' she said. 'We'll have enough lumber as it is.'

Malachey began to rake the dimming fire, shovelling the ashes into an empty cardboard box which had once held Golden Syrup tins.

'Listen,' he murmured, holding up the shovel. The strainings of a melodeon came faintly through the walls, together with the sound of a man singing. 'Jackie Murphy with his melodeon, and old Mick.'

'Lord, they're terrible people for music, the Murphys,' Kelly said, 'aren't they? Just like them, isn't it, to sit there playing and singing with the water up round the door?'

They stood quite still, their heads slightly raised, listening to the sweet berling of the music and the deep, lively voice of old Mick, as he tramped through the kitchen.

> Mush, mush, mush, tur-il i-addy
> And a mush, mush, tur-il i-ay
> Oh if you're in for a row or a ruction
> Just tread on the tail of me coat.

Neilly awoke suddenly out of a sound sleep. He lay still for a moment, feeling very wide awake. The room was quite dark, the fire almost out; it stirred faintly now and then, baring tiny, red glimmers, pinpoints, that pierced the blackness, but did not melt it. He looked over in the direction of Eugene's bed, in which Pachy and Johnny Kelly were lying, as his mother, at the heels of the hunt, would not let them leave after all. Eugene was in with Shemie and himself, and he had been crushed over to the very edge. He tried now to worm back a little, but Shemie, in the middle, could not be stirred.

He relaxed, lying as he had lain earlier that morning, his ears straining to catch every sound, pressing through the outer noise-husk of rain and breathing in quest of the inaudible.

He squeezed out gently from beneath the sheets and tiptoed to the head of the stairs, pulling his shirt down where it had gathered round the sticky, warm skin of his back. He felt his way slowly down, blinking his eyes tightly against the darkness. A faint gleam of water showed and he stopped, his heart racing madly.

He bent down and stirred the coldness with his hand. The water tinkled faintly and, in his imagination, he saw the silken ripples beating gently through the kitchen, beating softly over the surface of the flood through the dark silence, widening and fading. The dark, and the silence, and the cold black water! The picture scared him. His eyes watered, and he ran quickly back up the stairs.

He paused again at the head and then, suddenly, an unbearable happiness surged up within him. He shivered and hugged his arms about his chest, twisting his body, and giggling deeply and soundlessly in his throat. He knew that, because of the flood, he would not have to go to school for a day or so, but his sudden happiness went deeper than that. He did not seek to find the reason. He only knew that their house was flooded, that they had not gone to bed until nearly twelve o'clock last night, that Eugene was sleeping in his bed, and that his uncle Pachy and Johnny Kelly were lying over there in the corner in Eugene's; that he could now turn a bicycle on the road, without having to get off, that – He glanced once again down the stairs, and darted back to bed.

6

Neilly filled both buckets almost to the brim, and set them out on the path. His right arm ached from the screwing of the pump handle, and he stood for a moment flexing it slowly up and down, and probing his fingers into the turgid, sinewy bicep, tensing and relaxing underneath his jersey.

The vast bulk of the Mill spread before him, silent and deserted against the blue sky. The only movement about it was that made by a piece of grey tow, flapping wearily from the corner of the roof; and by a wisp of smoke, curling listlessly from the great chimney out into clear sunny air. A feeling akin to sadness came over him. It was as if the Mill were some living thing with thoughts and with feelings of its own – a monster, not evil, but downcast and lonely. In his imagination the slow, curving smoke, and the dangling twist of tow, became its final, hopeless appeals to the workers who had left. Their going had been abrupt and cruel, and the reason was beyond its understanding.

He sighed and looked down at the buckets, noticing the faint yellowy-green tint that the water imparted to the enamel. If he could get them down to the house now, like that, brave and full, without spilling too much, maybe his mother would let Shemie and him go to the pictures after all. Sure, just because they had been to Confession – He couldn't see what harm just going to the pictures would do. He bent down to grasp the handles. Then he straightened himself again. But wait! Maybe they were too full. If he came in with the water slopping all round him, and his stockings and shoes wringing, that would only aggravate his mother even more. Maybe he should throw a wee drop out? No! Any he threw out he'd be glad of when he got down to the house. He'd go easy, but wouldn't throw any out.

He set an imaginary mark about an inch from the brim of each bucket. He'd see if he could carry them down without spilling more than that much.

Very carefully he started off down the path, towards the stile. Between darting glances at the buckets, he kept his eyes trained on the path, avoiding the rough parts lest the slightest jolt of his foot should stir up a wave. At the stile he carried each bucket over separately, hardly daring to breathe, until they were deposited in safety on the smooth road beyond.

As he was coming down past the thick grey stone wall of the Mill yard, three boys came trotting round the Corner of the Row. At their hail, Neilly looked up, hurriedly smoothing the grimace of exertion from his face. He straightened himself with an effort and began to whistle, trying to appear as though he could hardly feel the weight of the buckets at all.

The eldest of the three boys, Devlin, dropped into a long, menacing stride as he came up. He humped his shoulders over, and hung his hands poised over his hips. He bore the nickname of the Preacher, after the notorious Western-magazine gunman.

'Howdy, amigo?' he leered.

Suddenly his expression changed from amiability to hatred, and his hands swooped towards his hips.

'Get outa town, pardner,' he snarled. 'The sheriff's on your trail!'

Neilly stood holding on to the buckets for a moment for appearance sake. Then he lowered them, slowly and with exquisite relief.

'Are you getting going, Neilly?' one of the other boys asked.

'Ah, I don't know,' Neilly answered doubtfully. 'She says it's a sin to go to the pictures after Confession.'

'How is it a sin? I asked the priest.'

'Well, that's what she says.'

'Hurry on down and ask her again. We'll walk slow.'

Neilly bent towards the buckets again.

'If you're allowed, run up quick. You'll catch us on the Asylum Hill.' The boys walked on, and the Preacher shouted: 'Adios, amigo. I'll fill you full of lead.' His shout spiralled into a scream. 'I am the bravest man in all Mexico – Ai-e-e-e-e –'

Neilly came on smiling, in spite of his longing to be with them. There was a powerful picture on, but he knew that his mother would hardly let them go now. At the Corner, he was forced to rest again. He felt pleased with himself, for the water was still lapping around the rims. He gave his arms a bit of a rub and took several deep breaths. This would be his last stop. Could he make it all the way down? The thought of the pictures faded for the moment. Yes! This time it was do or die. He had never been able to accomplish this feat before. Always on his way round from the pump at this halt at the Corner, there took place this same bitter marshalling of strength and resolve. Each time it was, 'This time it is do or die,' but up till now it had been 'die'. Connelly's door, four above his own, represented the limit of his penetration. Here it was, and sometimes before, that his arms and shoulders called out their final excruciating shriek, a cry that could not have been denied even for the tiniest fraction of another moment, for all the riches of the earth. But this time – this time it was do or die!

He stepped gingerly off the cribben, crossed the street, and up onto the high cribben on the other side. He paid attention to the children playing, or to the group of fellows standing against the Dining Room arguing. One young girl began skipping round him. In a sudden fury he roared at her, and she ran off with a cry.

He was only halfway down. Already he felt like dropping the buckets. His lips were twisted into a snarl of pain. A woman leaning over a half-door spoke to him as he passed, but he scarcely heard her. The water began to slop over. He tried desperately to steady himself, but the water seemed to have become imbued with a mischievous life of its own. Despite his efforts it persisted in dancing maddeningly out over his shoes and stockings.

A grunt of anguish escaped him, and in despair he stopped and lowered the buckets. The relief that swept through his arms sweetened his failure. He began to make excuses for himself. The buckets were far too full anyway! And he had screwed that ould pump handle round too quickly; that had tired his arm too much. How could anyone expect him to carry two full buckets of water, all the way down there, after wringing at that ould handle till he could barely move? But the next time. He'd do it the next time. One last great attempt.

He brushed the wet from his stockings and stamped his shoes against the ground. There wasn't much spilled after all, they were brave and full yet. Next time. Grasping the handles once again he moved on down.

The door of his own house was lying ajar, and he shouldered his way in. His mother came forward.

'Mind now, mind yourself. Don't spill it. Why do you take them so full?'

Neilly accepted the last remark as a compliment, and proudly handed the buckets over. His father was sitting in the armchair reading the *Irish News*. Shemie was hunched up on the old sofa, scowling and knuckling his tear-blackened eyes.

Kitty came up the hall, and Neilly returned tentatively to the attack.

'Mammy –'

'What-ey?'

'Mammy, Petey Devlin and the boys are away to the pics. They said they'd walk slow, and we could catch them up if you'd –'

'Now look,' said Kitty, her voice rising, 'I don't want to hear any more talk about the pictures. How many times must I tell you you're not going?'

A whine crept into Neilly's voice.

'Ah, Mammy, go on. I got the water for you. The priest told Jackie Devine, so he did, that it wasn't any harm.'

'I don't care if the Pope told Jackie Devine. I'm telling you –'

Malachey rustled at his paper.

'Ah, for God's sake let them run on, and not have the house in an uproar.'

Kitty turned on him.

'What have I said? Have I spoken? I see plainly that it's no use talking here at all. I told them the last time that they weren't going to the pictures any more after Confession. You must think I'm only here for an ornament or something.'

'Ah-h-h!'

Shemie, seeing the last hope beginning to ebb, started to cry again. Kitty grabbed him by the shoulder and pushed him through the red curtains, out behind the counter.

'Here,' she said, 'out you go. I'm not going to have you sitting there crying bad luck about the place. Hell run picture day be about you! When I was your age I was thankful if I had a cut of dry bread, without whingeing about going to the pictures.'

She pushed Neilly out as well and then, going over to the window, brought out a handful of sweets which she flung after them into the hall.

'Away now, and divert yourselves in the good fresh air like other childer.'

Desolate though the boys were, it did not prevent a scramble for the sweets. Making sure that they had picked them all up, and that none had tumbled in behind the door, they trailed out into the street, arguing now about who got the most.

'You did!' Shemie accused. 'I only got five. Look.'

'Well, that's your own fault,' said Neilly. 'It was a scramble, wasn't it?' Then he relented at the sight of his brother's tear-streaked face, and he gave him another three caramels. 'Quit crying! What's the use of crying now? No pics the day.'

Shemie could not be comforted. He hung around the door, as though still hoping against hope for a last-minute softening of heart from within, and, after a final exhortation to come on, Neilly left him and went walking up the Row. Once he looked behind and grinned, as, just in time, he saw Shemie give a spring away from the door, as it was suddenly pulled open again. His mother leaned out and angrily waved the younger boy away. With many truculent, backward glances, he came slithering up after Neilly.

At the Corner, Neilly took a stand against the Dining Room window. Bending his knees, he slowly sank onto his hunkers. The sun shone down on him warmly, and his mouth was filled with the soft, cloying sweetness of the caramel he was eating. He kept grazing his teeth over the smooth, sucked surface. He made a series of little dents in it with his front teeth and scraped his tongue along the tiny ridges. He longed to sink his teeth down in the first delicious bite, and to feel the spurt of the thick, sweet juice under his tongue. He shivered with delight and then, pushing the caramel gently between his teeth, he closed his eyes and bit slowly through the middle. He started chewing ravenously. Shemie came up and leaned against the wall beside him.

An argument was going on between a dozen or so of the big fellows, standing round the door. Tommy Kelly, Johnny's brother, was holding forth as usual.

'Now look, if God put a man on this earth to commit a murder, why should the law punish that man? Why should the law hold a man responsible for something which he was put on the earth to do?'

'Ah, talk sense, man. How could God put anyone on the earth to commit a murder?'

'Well, it's the same thing, isn't it – if you believe in fate? That's what fate means, doesn't it? That everything is left out for you. And if everything is left out for you, then answer my question! Why should a man be hung for something that he's put on this earth to do?'

'Ah-h-h-'

'Ah, it's all right ah-h-h-. But you can't answer my question.'

An old man, wearing an old pair of trousers with the legs narrow as drainpipes, came strolling up smoking an old clay pipe. He lifted his pipe and hocked a big brown clougher out into the road.

'What the blazes are you blethering about now, Kelly?' he grunted. 'Does that ould tongue of yours never cease? I don't care when I come up to this Corner, I'm always sure to find you here arguing the toss.'

Kelly appealed to him with outstretched hands.

'Well look, I'll leave it up to you now, Ned. What do you say about it? Do you believe in fate?'

'Fate! Fate!' Old Ned spat out the word in sardonic contempt. 'And what, in God's holy name, will you tell us now, does that mean?'

'Don't tell me that you don't know what fate means.'

'Well, tell us you what it means. Fate!'

'My God, anybody can tell you what fate means – Well, it means that – what I mean is, do you believe that everything that you do is left out for you to do?'

'Of course I do, man dear,' old Ned shot back fiercely. 'What are you talking about? Look up at the ould Mill. Look at her sitting up there, hell to her soul; sure, there's the proof for you, if you only had the wit to open your eyes.'

Kelly was a little taken aback at this.

'What? What has the Mill got to do with it?'

'God a God, you're a shocking man, Kelly, altogether. I suppose you think, like a lot of other people, that St Patrick' – old Ned gave another big spit – 'once built a chapel here, do you?'

'Of course he did. Sure, anybody knows that. St Patrick –'

'St Patrick your grandmother,' old Ned snarled. 'I'm surprised to hear you talking like that, Kelly, and St Patrick's Day itself only a day or two off. Are you an Irishman at all? St Patrick! St Patrick was going to build some sort of a chapel here, I'll give you that, but sure isn't it in the history books that he went into a terrible huff over it, because he couldn't get the snakes out of the Row there? Out of every other part of Ireland he got them shot, but hell roast the foot, would they stir from here, and at the heels of the hunt he got into such a crab over the head of it all, that in place of the Chapel he stuck up an ould mill instead and, says he, now this'll be the greatest ould curse of a mill for going on and off that'll ever be heard tell of.'

Old Ned waved his hand.

'Yes, there she stands. Look at her. Take a good look now. There she is, sitting up there to this very day, no sooner on till she's off, and no sooner off till she's on, and vicey versy. Sure, isn't it a face that the people could hardly get into the cathedral all last week to say their prayers with ould Mrs Grimes and ould Ellen Taggert, and all the ould dolls in the Row, all lighting candles and making Novenas to St Patrick? Sure, I believe they near set the altar afire last Thursday there. But still an' all, didn't she go off just the same, didn't she? And you're standing there blethering about fate! What the hell's that? Isn't that fate?'

The fellow laughed with delight. There were cries of: 'Ah, bould Ned there! Good man there, Ned, that's the stuff!'

The old man lashed another venomous mouthful out into the street.

Kelly reddened and gaped at him. He swung round angrily, and kicked the toe of his boot into the ground. He started to say something, but just at that moment a series of screams, mingled with the snarling and barking of a dog, broke out round the Corner towards the Bridge wall. The fellows all jerked round. They saw a dirty-looking mongrel snapping viciously at the bare legs of a young girl. Several other young girls danced about, shrieking fearfully.

Three boys were shouting at the dog and striving to pull or beat it away.

One of them, a lad in a loose red jersey about three sizes too big for him, succeeded at last in getting a grip on the mongrel's hind legs, and he trailed it back, panting. The little girl fled, and one of the fellows caught her by the elbows.

'What's the matter? You're all right, he didn't bite you. Don't be crying, you're all right, you're all right.'

Tommy Kelly rushed round, his face white with rage. He made a savage lunge at the dog, but the boy caught it up in his arms and hugged it, squirming and yelping, to his chest.

'Ah, Daddy, don't, don't!' he cried.

Kelly gave him a cuff on the ear that nearly knocked him over.

I thought I told you to keep that dog in the house; am I talking to myself? Take it away down there to hell out of that, and don't let me see either you or it outside the house the day more. I'm not warning you again now. Go on!'

It's not the dog's fault,' the boy sobbed. 'How is it he never bites me? We were just coming up the road there, and them wee yaaps started calling it names.' His eyes suddenly flashed with rage, and he shouted over at the young girls: 'Why don't yez leave the dog alone? The next time I get yez near it –' He choked with fury, and his father gave him another wallop.

'Go on, big fellow. When I see that Johnny fellow of yours again, I'll get him to bring it back to where he found it, wherever the hell that was.'

The boy trailed away weeping, still carrying the dog, despite its struggling. Kelly turned to the fellows.

'Eh! That's a dog and a half for you. A wicked ould carn!'

They turned back to the Corner again.

From the top of the Asylum wall, two or three lads, who had clambered up, beckoned eagerly.

'Here's the patients, here's the patients,' they cried.

The boys on the road dashed over and began clambering excitedly up beside them. The smaller boys, who could not make the climb, danced in anguish on the cribben, shouting for a hand up. Neilly pulled Shemie, and a few of the others, up beside him, and they all juked through the fir trees to where a column of patients, four or five abreast, were approaching down the walk alongside the wall. As they drew near, some of the boys took fright and swung round on their stomachs, ready for a quick drop back onto the road.

The patients were dressed in rough grey suits and caps, and were shepherded by a tall, blue-uniformed keeper. The boys began to call out greetings. Some of the men glanced over with blank, sullen faces, and a tall, thin man, who was walking out in front of the rest, with his arms folded, turned his head and spat viciously up at them. Others smiled, waved, and shouted back. Then, with amazing suddenness, a little man darted out from the ranks, and made an eel-like leap towards Neilly's leg. The boys screamed. Neilly jerked his leg up and twisted round onto his stomach. The little man sniggered up at them.

'Any fegs?' he whispered. 'Any fegs, any tobacco? Throw us down some fegs.'

The boys rifled their pockets, and tossed down their odds and ends, stubs of pencils, cigarette cards and so forth.

'No fegs,' they shouted. 'Bring you some fegs the morrow. No fegs the day.'

The little man grinned with delight. He jumped up, snatching at the bright, fluttering cigarette cards, and two other men rushed over and joined in the scramble. The keeper came running up, and ushered the patients back into the batch.

In a fury he started flinging stones at the boys, forcing them to a descent so precipitous that they had not even time to shout back a single name. They gathered round the wall, undecided as to their next move. Then they saw a crowd of the big fellows coming round the Corner, one of them tossing up a bullet.

'There's a score starting, boys,' Neilly called, and they raced up eagerly to see the first shots being broken.

7

The boys followed the score out and got back to the Corner about five o'clock. A few old men were standing up against the Dining Room wall, smoking. Pachy and Johnny Kelly were standing with them, and down at their door was Johnny Kelly's donkey and cart. The donkey was munching hungrily at an armful of hay strewn on the ground.

'Hello, Pachy,' Neilly greeted, 'we were down at the score there.'

'Ah, were you? Where's the banty?'

'Who? Shemie?' Neilly glanced around him. 'I dunno. He must be round at the Bridge wall.'

Pachy turned to the bullet man.

'Well, who won all the money?' he asked.

An argument then started up regarding the shots which had been played. Tommy Kelly, the losing man's marker, pointed out that, if his man had played the shots properly, the way he had shown, the score would have been a walkover. He put his hands out, and began to illustrate his point.

'Now that shot from the pole on top of the hill –'

The rest of the fellows tightened their lips at each other. 'Ah, now –' Neilly, too, smiled up at Pachy, anxious to share in their ironic tolerance. Just then he noticed the Preacher and the two other boys he had met, coming down again into his long, menacing stride, and lifted his hands, pointing out his forefingers.

'Don't make a move,' he called. 'You're covered!'

'Well, well,' said Pachy, 'by the blinking left! Look who's here. Buck Jones himself.'

'I ain't Buck Jones, pardner,' the Preacher snarled. 'I bumped that guy off weeks ago.'

The fellows laughed.

'Well, well, well,' Pachy mused. 'So poor old Buck Jones has bit the dust. What did you bump off a decent guy like that for? I hear Billy the Kid's on the trail looking for the guy that done it.'

The Preacher made another lightning draw, and backed a few paces, his eyes glancing quickly from side to side.

'The Kid,' he grated, 'so the Kid's in town, eh? I'll give him to sundown to hit the trail. After that, there's liable to be a lot of lead flying around.'

He let out a shout, and galloped off down the Row, slapping his hand against his hip.

'Sundown! I'll give him to sundown.'

Pachy turned and laughed.

'Why don't you jump on your horse like that, Neilly, and away down and lift us a few old Woodbines? I'm choking for a draw.'

'What? Pinch them?'

'What d'you mean, pinch them? You don't think that Tom Mix there would ask a question like that, d'you? Throw your leg over your horse there.'

Neilly hesitated, torn between his desire to please Pachy and the natural prickings of his conscience.

'I was at Confession the day,' he demurred. 'Only for that –'

'Ah, what harm is there in a mingy Woodbine? Shemie would go if he was here. Where's Shemie? He'll go Christ the night! A poor pal you're turning out to be.'

Neilly hesitated for a few moments longer. Then he cantered off uneasily.

'Tell Kitty they're for Ken Maynard, if she sees you,' Pachy called after him.

Some of the fellows smiled and shook their heads.

'You'll have Kitty out on the warpath. Wait'll you see, he'll be caught.'

Pachy watched Neilly disappear into the shop. He laughed again, but did not speak. About two minutes passed, and Neilly came shooting out again.

'Ah, good man,' said Pachy, 'here it is.'

But the next moment Kitty appeared in the doorway and shouted after him.

Neilly stopped, and the fellows saw him gaze despairingly up at them. Then, as his mother called again: 'Neilly, I want you. Come back here this minute.' He turned and was hauled back into the house by the butt of the ear.

The fellows all began to move about very self-consciously, clearing their throats noisily and scraping their hands together.

'Why didn't he come on up?' said Pachy. 'The wee fool. He's destroyed now.'

'Why don't you go for a nice dander down the road, Pachy?' some wit suggested. 'God bless us, a lovely evening like that.'

But Pachy was unruffled.

'No-o-o! What do I want to go down the road for a walk for? I've been walking all day.'

At that moment Kitty reappeared in the doorway and shook her fist up.

'It's a wonder you aren't ashamed of yourself, sending the childer down to stale cigarettes. I'll get the police,' she called.

Pachy cast his eyes up.

'Ah, bould Kate there!'

Kitty withdrew again, and Pachy shrugged his shoulders.

'Well, I suppose I'd better go on down and see what all the blinking shouting's about. Kate takes these notions sometimes, you know.'

He stuck his hands in his pockets and sauntered down, whistling, into the shop. Kitty came to meet him in the hall.

'Is this a new trick now? Well, a nice fellow you're turning out to be. For two pins I wouldn't think much of putting my coat on and getting you lifted. If this is all you're ever going to do with yourself?'

Pachy pursed up his lips, and juking through the curtains he saw Teasie sitting on the sofa. Malachey was leaning against the mantelpiece in his shirtsleeves, smoking. Pachy breathed a sigh of relief. He gave an innocent smile.

'Why, what's wrong? What's the matter?' He came on into the kitchen. 'Hello, Teresa, you're a bit of a stranger. How's the old woman? Malachey!'

Malachey tightened his lips at him and shook his head. His expression said: 'Well, you've done it this now. The fat's in the fire this time.'

The two packets of Woodbines were lying on the counter, and over by the window Neilly was standing, snuffling.

'What's up?' Pachy asked again. 'What's all the narration about?'

'Ah, now,' Kitty sighed, 'God help us! God help us. That's all I can say. When you have to send a young innocent child down to stale cigarettes for you, well – God help us! That's all I can say.'

Pachy rocked back on his heels, to and fro, gently.

'I'm afraid you've got things a wee bit mixed up, Kate. Neilly, did I send you down here to stale cigarettes?'

Neilly looked at him with his left eye covered by his fist.

'What did I say?' Pachy asked him. 'Who did I say they were for?'

Neilly hesitated.

'You said you wanted them for Ku – Ken Maynard.'

Pachy looked around him and spread his hands out.

'Well, what harm was there in that? I only asked him to jump on his horse and bring us up a loc of cigarettes. I didn't mean him to pinch them.'

'Well, there he stands,' Kitty said, shortly. 'And now he won't be able to go near the altar in the morning. That's the Confession for you, and all about it.'

'Ah, sure let him say a good Act of Contrition, and God won't say another word about it. Sure he didn't mean anything. He only picked me up the wrong way.' Pachy moved over and rubbed his hands over Neilly's head. 'Ah, he's not a bad fellow. The only kid in the house! What are you? Ha-ha! The only kid in the house!' He looked over at Malachey. 'Believe there was a good score there the day, Malachey. You didn't go? Blinking fool you, you might have lifted a few bob. How's Tommy keeping, Teasie? I haven't seen him for a couple of days.'

Teasie recrossed her legs.

'Aye, Tommy!'

Pachy moved out round the counter again.

'Coming up to the Corner, Malachey? Get on your coat there, man dear.' He reached over towards the cigarettes. 'Can you spare these, Kate? I'll bring you in an old rooster when it gets dark.'

Kitty went over and pulled the drawer open.

'Where's Kelly? Is he up there?' She threw out another two packets. 'I suppose he hasn't a butt either. Don't you be going too far now, Malachey, the tay'll soon be ready.'

'Aye, right,' Malachey grunted.

'Well, cheerio, Teasie. Tell the old woman I'll be over for a drink of her aleplant one of these days. Cheerio, Kate.'

'Aye, cheerio! Cheerio!'

'Cheerio!' Kitty repeated when they had gone. 'Cheerio, aye! That's the quare playboy for you! What in under God would you do with a fellow like that at all? I'm sick, sore and tired trying to talk some sense into him. But ah-h-h – I wish to God he'd stayed in the army.'

'Ah, poor Pachy.' Teasie smiled. 'How do they knock it out at all? Him and that Kelly fellow and his ould donkey and cart, and his rags and his jam pots. I feel a great pity sometimes for Johnny Kelly. He's lost over in that ould barrack ever since poor Annie died, God rest her.'

'Annie was good to Johnny,' Kitty murmured.

'There must have been a brave squad of them Kellys. Is the other girl of them still living in England? There were only the two sisters, weren't there?'

'Aye! Eileen is getting on well over there, I believe. Her man is a manager of some big place. She sent Johnny his fare over, many's a time, but heh – you can guess the way it went – here, where are you off to?'

Neilly was caught in the act of trying to edge round the counter. Kitty waggled her finger at him.

'Come on. In! In! Not another foot you'll stir outside that door the day. Sit down there and learn your Catechism, it'll answer you better. How you're going to kneel down at the altar in the morning I do not know. Where's that other ottercop?'

'I dunno where he is.'

'You dunno where he is! You dunno nothing! I wish to God I had let you run on to the pictures, away from about the place.'

'Ah, let him alone, God help him,' Teasie interceded. 'He's only a child yet.'

'A quare child! He's big and ugly enough to know what staling is.' Neilly began to sob softly again. 'Are you starting again?' Kitty demanded, threateningly. 'Have done now, this minute, this very minute, or I'm telling you I'll give you something to cry for. God's truth, I think you got off very lightly indeed. Let me see you sitting down there now with your Catechism and – don't wipe your nose on the sleeve of your jersey. God bless us, but I hate to see anybody doing that. Where's your handkerchief?'

Teasie held her own out to him.

'Here, son, don't cry now, like a good boy. Ah, Lord, Kitty, you're too hard on them sometimes. That's the boy! Don't be crying now, sure there's nothing to cry about.'

Neilly went sniffling into the room and brought his school-bag out.

'Well, look here,' said Kitty, glancing up at the clock, 'you can go out for a half an hour, no more. Be back here at six o'clock.'

Neilly wiped his fingers across his eyes and hiccuped gently. Without speaking, he walked through the curtains round the counter.

'Six o'clock, mind you,' Kitty called after him. She raised her voice. 'And keep away from that Pachy fellow.'

Teasie rose up.

'Well, I'll have to be going now myself, Kitty.' Her lips moved bitterly. 'If I stay any longer that'll be another fault.'

'Well, mind now what I said,' Kitty advised. 'I know the old woman is hard to put up with at times, but sure she's the best in the world really. Sure I wouldn't take under my notice anything she says, that's only her way of going on. That woman couldn't live if she hadn't someone to fight and argue with.'

'Ach, I know, Kitty, I know. I've got nothing against the ould doll. That's only her nature, I know. It's Tommy I blame. Lord God, we all know how good his mother is to him – Oh, the sun rises and sets on Tommy – but, after all, I'm his wife, and he should think of my position once in a while. He could put an end to it all, you know, this very minute himself, if he'd say, "Well, look now, Mother, I've married Teasie, and here she is, either for good or for ill, that remains to be seen, so why not try and make the best of it, and not be always bickering and –" But instead of that, he encourages her. Oh, maybe not on purpose! But he takes her part always, and you see, well, that makes her worse. Any argument that gets started – I'm the one who started it, and who the hell do I think I am, talking to his mother like that? His mother, his mother all the time. I'm telling you, Kitty, if it wasn't for the child I wouldn't stick it any longer. I – Who in the name o' God's that?'

A series of sharp kicks was suddenly delivered against the front door. Kitty opened it, and a little girl stumbled into the hall. She held up a penny in her grimy fist.

'A happorth o' sweets and a ha'penny back,' she chanted.

Kitty came back round the counter.

'What kind of sweets, daughter? Caramels?'

The child nodded gravely.

'A happorth o' caramels and a ha'penny back.'

Kitty put five caramels into a small paper bag and reached them over the counter. The little girl took them and held up her penny. 'And a ha'penny back.'

Teasie and Kitty followed her to the door, laughing.

'Mind the step now, daughter.'

They stood together for a few moments. Teasie was just about to move away when a terrible outburst of crying suddenly sounded from up at the Corner. As they looked up, a young boy came round in the Row, hurrying through the crowd of fellows, howling piteously.

'Sacred Heart of Jesus!' Kitty exclaimed. 'It's Shemie. He's fallen into the river again.'

They heard Malachey call out to him, as his father recovered from his astonishment, but Shemie came tottering on heedlessly, roaring at the top of his voice, and the water running out of him.

Malachey, Pachy and Neilly started after him, and here and there along both sides of the Row, heads popped out over the half-doors. Old women clicked their tongues and murmured their sympathy as Shemie passed.

'Ah, God help him, he's drownded. Hurry on home, son, quick.'

'Bring him down, Malachey,' Kitty called, 'bring him on down. Jesus, Mary and St Joseph, that young fellow will be drownded yet. That's the third time this month. Now you see what I have to put up with, Teasie. What unlucky prayer was hanging round my head this day that I didn't send them off to the pictures when I had the chance. Come on, come on! If I wouldn't be better off handcuffed to a ghost it's a quare thing to me.'

8

Teasie lifted the umbrella from the nail behind the door. She closed the door quietly behind her and tightened the shawl around the child in her arms. When she opened the umbrella, the rain drummed against it like a flurry of pebbles.

She walked quickly along the cribben. There was no one in sight except two young girls leaning over a half-door on the other side of the Row, chanting out at the rain. At the Corner she crossed the road and stood for a moment against the Asylum wall, looking back into the Row. Then she turned away slowly, on down the road, alongside the heavy, rain-darkened wall.

She took a deep breath of the rain-scented air. Oh, Mother of God, but she was glad to get out!

After dinner, just before the rain had come on again, Tommy had gone up the town to the Labour Bureau. Teasie was washing up the dinner things, when the old woman had got on to her about the water not being hot enough, and was she so stupid as to think that you could wash greasy dishes in half-cold water? Teasie had not said very much then, remembering Kitty's advice. Later, the old woman took a notion of washing the floor, despite the fact that it was quite clean, having been washed only two days ago, and that in any case it was starting to rain. Teasie had been sitting on the stool by the fire, nursing the child, and the old woman, spiteful from the argument, had washed her from one chair to the other until, at length, unable to endure it any longer, she had lapped the child in an old shawl and come out.

The child lay quietly in her arms, its eyelids drooping sleepily. Teasie pulled a corner of the shawl over its forehead. The child stared up at her, and she murmured: 'Go to sleep now. That's the good boy. Go to sleep.'

A man swept past on a bicycle, the tyres hissing over the wet road, and her gaze automatically followed him down, noticing in a detached way the hunch of his shoulders over the handlebars, and the flying tails of his coat. When he had passed out of sight, the loneliness and silence of the road seemed to deepen and press like a weight upon her heart.

'Oh, Mother of God!' she murmured aloud, 'how much longer is this going to last? How much longer am I going to be able to stay in that house?'

A little way past the end of the Asylum wall, she suddenly noticed a woman standing in against the hedge under a tree. The woman, like herself, was holding up an umbrella, and as Teasie drew nearer she could see her watching her curiously. She looked to be a woman of about fifty years of age, plump and well dressed, and apparently she was waiting for someone.

Teasie was just going to murmur the time of day to her, and pass on. But, as she came level, the woman leaned forward slightly, with a look of concern and pity in her eyes.

'In the name of God, daughter,' she said very gently, 'but where are you going on such a day as this?'

Teasie halted, startled and confused. She twisted the shawl tighter around the child, and for a moment did not know what to answer.

'Oh, I'm just going down the road for a walk,' she said.

The woman kept watching her closely.

'I hope you don't mind me speaking to you like this, daughter, but tell me, is there anything the matter? Is there anything troubling you?'

The woman's kindly face and voice allayed any resentment which Teasie might have otherwise felt.

'Oh, not at all, missus,' she replied, as casually as she could. 'There's nothing troubling me.'

'Are you sure now? Is that your own wee child, daughter?'

'Yes!'

'And are you married?'

Teasie nodded.

'And are you living with your man?'

'Oh, yes!' Teasie replied. 'My husband's with me all right.'

The woman regarded her doubtfully.

'Well, look, daughter, don't now, for God's sake, be offended at me speaking to you like this; believe me, it's not just out of curiosity. You're looking at a woman who has been through a lot of trouble herself, and, daughter dear, that something is very much the matter with you, is plain to be seen; for, daughter dear, it's writ all over your face. Are you sure there's nothing now that you'd like me to do for you? Don't be afraid, for, though I mightn't look it now, many's the hard and bitter tear, child, I have shed myself.'

Suddenly Teasie wanted to get away from her. She was touched by the woman's kind words, but realised the futility of talking any further. It would be impossible for her to open her heart to a stranger, however well-meaning, encountered on the road like this. The conversation, so far, had only increased her sense of desolation. Hurriedly, but calmly, she said: 'Well, missus, I'm sure you mean well, but I assure you that you are entirely mistaken about me. There is nothing the matter at all, indeed. I only just thought I'd take a wee stroll out, after sitting in the house all day. The umbrella'll save the child.'

Without waiting to give the woman a chance to say anything else, she moved on, but not too quickly, for she did not want to hurt the woman's feelings. She could sense the woman gazing after her, with her soft eyes, curious, sad, and kind. A motor car came around the corner and swept up past Teasie. She heard it slowing down behind her, and braking to a halt. She thought that the car must be what the woman had been waiting for, but did not look around. Then there came the sound of the car starting up again, and the dwindling swish of the tyres as it sped up the road.

Teasie walked on, with her head slightly bowed. Now and again she looked up, and glanced out slowly from under the umbrella, passing the tip of her tongue along her upper lip. She seemed to be deep in thought, meditating over the little encounter which had just taken place. In reality her mind was almost completely devoid of thought of any kind. A soft, dreamy haze seemed to envelop her mind and body. She walked without any conscious effort. Her mind seemed almost asleep. She thought dimly that she could keep on walking like this for miles and miles, miles and miles . . .

The Asylum clock was striking five as she was passing the Bridge wall. It was still raining steadily, and she tightened the shawl once again round the child in her arms. The child slept on, lying warm and snug in the shawl, quite dry under the umbrella. The Row stretched empty and desolate, and Teasie hurried down, glad that there was nobody about; the two little girls, who had been singing out at the rain when she left, were no longer in sight, and every door along both sides was shut tight. At her own door, Teasie paused for a moment to lower her umbrella. Then, without any further hesitation, she pressed down upon the latch and pushed on in.

The hot, sweet smell of freshly baked soda farls rushed into her nostrils. As she wiped her feet on the bag lying in the hall, the old woman, cap on the back of her head, looked round from where she was bending over the pan on the fire. Tommy was sitting in his waistcoat, in the armchair. His legs were crossed and thrust out straight in front of him, so that the old woman had to bend away over every time she came to the pan. His right elbow was resting on the arm of the chair, and he was twisting a lock of hair round and round on his finger and thumb.

Teasie hung the umbrella quietly back on its hook behind the door and, as she came on in, the old woman turned back wordlessly to the pan. She lifted off the four triangular farls and carried them over to the table. In passing, she happened to glance down at the floor, and noticed the shocking condition of Teasie's shoes. She stiffened, and the old head shook angrily.

'How did your shoes get in that state? Can you not walk a few doors up the Row without ploughing into the puddles?'

'Oh, for God's sake, let me get into the house,' Teasie shot back instantly.

The child woke, and began to whimper, and she laid it in the pram in the room. Going down the back hall, she poured some milk into a small saucepan. She came back into the kitchen and set the saucepan gently on the glowing coals, beneath the baking pan hanging from the chimney-hook. She did not look at Tommy, no more than if he was not there at all.

The old woman glanced round sourly.

'What are you going to do now?'

Teasie set her lips and grunted.

'What am I going to do? What do you think I'm going to do? The child's hungry.'

'It might be a good idea to get those shoes off. Look at the state of the floor already, and me only after washing it. Dambut, you'd think that you were a big child or something, that you can't stay out of the puddles.'

Teasie caught hold of the edge of the fire-board with her right hand. For a moment she did not speak. She stood frowning and chewing at the inside of her lower lip, as if some vague and yet important thought, far removed from the present issue, had just occurred to her. Then she said: 'Will you tell me what puddles you're talking about, or what are you talking about, for I can't make head nor tail of it! What puddles did I go into? I don't remember going near any puddles. I can't seem to recollect at all.' She spoke with a calculated and deliberate puzzlement, as if it were all part of a game she was having with a very young child.

The old woman's face flushed. Without answering, she turned back to the bake-board, and began kneading the dough bad-temperedly.

Then Teasie dropped her pose and said: 'Good God Almighty, can I not go down the road for a walk without being accused of splashing through the puddles?'

The old woman still said nothing. Suddenly she turned around. It was as if what Teasie said had just penetrated her mind.

'You went down the road? You went down the road? Surely you don't mean to say that you took the child down the road for a walk, of a day like that?'

She rushed across the kitchen, and lifted the child from the pram and began racing her hands over it, feeling its shoulders, back and legs.

'Tsk! Tsk! Tsk! You take the child out of a day like that, and then come back and throw it into the pram. This child's drenched, soaking, wringing. You'll kill the child yet, before all's over, maybe you'll be satisfied then. Christ help us, what kind of an ould half-eegot are you anyway, or what do you mean to do? Here, come and feel this child, Tommy, just now . . .'

The milk boiled over suddenly, rising over the saucepan in a foamy cloud and flooding out into the fire. Teasie snatched quickly at the saucepan and set it on the hob. The handle seared her fingers, and she rubbed them over her dress, up and down her leg. She turned on the old woman, her eyes filled with bitterness and contempt.

'What are you gabbling about?' she asked quietly. 'Are you deliberately trying to drive me insane? You know as well as I do that there's not a tint of water on that child.'

Her voice rose. 'How in under the great God could any rain get onto the child, when I had the big umbrella over him all the time? Surely not even you would think that I'd bring a child out of a day like that without something of some sort over it?'

'That'll do now, that'll do now!' Tommy spoke up for the first time. 'There's no call to get sarcastic over it now. That'll do.'

'Sarcastic!' Teasie echoed. 'Christ! I think I have a right to get any way I like over it. I sat here in that chair there this day till I couldn't sit for another instant. That woman there, your mother, drove me out, and if that child had a got wet' – her eyes narrowed and she shook her head – 'oh, God, forgive me for saying it, but I almost wish it had a got soaked, and that something would have happened to it, because there's the woman who would have been responsible! That woman standing there, a woman who I know God will never allow to put one foot inside the holy gates of heaven because of the way that she has tortured and tormented me.'

Tommy's face swelled and reddened. He lifted his clenched fist very slowly and deliberately.

'By the eternal God you've asked for this. That's my mother you're talking about,' he said.

Teasie rushed over to the table and picked up a long dough-caked knife. She held it up before her.

'Just well darr you now! Just well darr you! Set one finger on me, boy, and that'll be the rock you'll perish on. You'll get this in you to the hilt, and we'll see what your mother'll be able to do for you then. Go on, set one finger on me if you darr.'

The old woman burst into sobs. She laid the child on the sofa, wiping her fingers over her eyes.

'I'll leave this house,' she wept. 'I'll go. I'll not stay here and have you at each other's throats over me. I'll go from this house, and I'll never come back.'

Before Tommy could stop her, she had rushed out through the door, and onto the street. Through the window they could see her huddling over towards Kitty's. The child lay howling on the sofa, but no one paid any attention to it.

For a moment neither Tommy nor Teasie moved or spoke, but stood looking at each other. Then Teasie shrugged her shoulders and tossed the knife back onto the table.

'Well,' she said, 'there's no use in her leaving. It's my place to go. This is her house.'

Tommy still did not move or speak. He stood in the centre of the kitchen, like someone in a daze, as if what had just taken place had happened too quickly for his mind to follow. Teasie lifted the child from the sofa, and hugged it to her, clapping it gently on the back. Her cheeks were flushed, and her eyes shone. Her face wore an expression almost of exaltation. She did not clearly know where she was going or what she was going to do, but she was glad that things had now come to a head. It was impossible to stay here any longer. Something would turn up. She was strong and healthy. She could work. Her and the child, with the help of God, they would always get what would do them.

She went to the door to take her coat from the hook. Footsteps sounded outside, and she heard Kitty's voice. She stepped back, the latch clicked, the door swung open, and Kitty came in with the old woman behind her. The old woman had a coat crowled over her shoulders, and as they came into the hall, Kitty trailed it off, and threw it over the end of the banisters. She did not have any such protection herself, and her thick auburn hair was speckled with raindrops.

'Go on in there now,' she said to the old woman, 'and sit down, and say nothing. What in the name of God has come over this house?' she asked Teasie. 'Why can you not live together in peace, like Christians, and not be making yourselves the laughing-stock of the Row? Lord God, if I were in your shoes I'd be ashamed – ashamed.'

With her coat over the crook of her left arm, Teasie followed her into the kitchen. Her right arm was clasped tightly around the child, petting it gently on the back.

'Tommy, I thought you had more sense,' Kitty accused.

'You know that your mother's heart is not in very good order, but still. What is the matter with this house anyway? Is there not enough fighting and arguing going on in the world? God knows you'll be far enough away from each other yet.'

'I'll kill that one, Kitty,' Tommy said, white to the lips. 'As sure as God's in heaven I'll kill that one yet.'

'H'm,' said Teasie. 'You had that chance there a couple of minutes ago. I wonder why you didn't go ahead then?'

'Shut up now, I'm telling you –'

The old woman, who had seated herself on the sofa, broke into tears again.

'I'll go,' she kept sobbing. 'I'll stay no more here, and have you fighting over me. I'll go.'

'Now, there's no use starting to cry over it again that I can see,' said Kitty. 'A lot of good that'll do anybody.'

'There'll be no call for you to go,' Teasie said coldly. 'This is your house, and I'm the one who's going to do the going. I wouldn't stay in this house for another hour, not if you were to hand me down the moon.'

'I'm glad to hear it,' Tommy grunted. 'I'm glad to hear it, but the child stays! You're not taking the child.'

Without a word, Teasie went into the room and put the child in the pram.

'There's your child,' she said. 'There's your child, and now we'll see how you'll get on with it for a change. The dog's life that I've got over that wee child, Kitty, you wouldn't believe it. If the milk's not too warm it's too cold, and if it's not too cold it's too hot, and because I took it out for a wee walk the day, and me and it as good as swept out, the uproar there was when I came back you'd have thought I murdered it.'

She pointed to the old woman sitting huddling on the sofa.

'God forgive me and pardon me for saying it, Kitty, but that woman there is bad, bad, bad! I've tried to make allowances, and to mind what you said, that it was only her way of going on, and that she didn't really mean it, but the haraking, Kitty, that that woman has given me on the day, and every day, since I had the misfortune to come into this house at all' – tears rushed into her eyes – 'well, all I can say is that it's the mercy of God Himself that I'm not over there in the Asylum, walking round the walks with a grey skirt on me, and my arms folded, that's all I can say. A woman with a kind face stopped me down at the Rhubarb Gate the day, a woman that I've never set eyes on before nor she on me, but who has more kindness in one corner of her heart than there'll ever be in this house in a hundred years. This woman stopped me at the Rhubarb Gate the day, and asked me if I was in trouble of some sort. She could see the lines of what I've been through writ and re-writ over my face. If a strange woman could see that, a woman who had never set eyes on me before, nor I on her, if a strange woman could see that, why couldn't he there? He knows the way I was being tortured here! Yet, instead of lifting his hand to help me – oh yes, he lifted his hand all right. I'll give him that much, oh yes! But wait, there's no use talking any more, out of this house I'm going the day, and it'll be a happy, happy day for me, I'm telling you, to have seen the last of it.'

She thrust her arms into the sleeves of her coat and shrugged it round her shoulders. In the room the child was crying in the pram. Kitty went and lifted it.

'Now, Teasie,' Kitty said, 'now don't be foolish now, and rush off, and do something that you'll regret. Your home's here, and your child's here, and what's the use –'

'Regret!' Teasie caught up the word and laughed. 'Regret! That's a good one. Don't argue with me now, Kitty, you've always been a good friend to me, and out of this godforsaken hole you're the only one I'll be sorry to leave. But it's no use arguing with me, for up my mind is made, and I've got, at least, the consolation of knowing that what has happened has happened through no fault of mine. My home's here, and my child's here, Kitty, as you've said, a poor home it has been to me, but thanks and praise be to God that nobody can say behind my back, or up to my face, that I left through any fault of my own. You're witness to that, Kitty. I've been driven out, and well that man standing there knows it. I'm glad this happened the day, so I am; it would have been the madhouse for me if I had stayed here much longer. I can work, thank God, and I can stay with Matty at the station till I get a position somewhere. And don't think for a moment I intend leaving the child here for good. God forbid that any innocent child should be left in this house. But just as soon as I can get a position somewhere I'll be back here for it. And let anyone try to keep it from me!'

She snatched an old brown beret from a nail on the banisters, and rushed out into the hall. Kitty shouted her name and tried to grab her, but she was out through the door in a flash, and up the footpath through the puddles as fast as she could put one leg past the other.

Later that evening, about nine o'clock, Tommy came up for her to her sister Matty.

'You'd better come on home, girl,' he said, his face dark and quiet, 'that child's in convulsions, and no one can get it pacified.'

Well, he didn't waste much time, did he, till he was after her? And what was wrong with the old woman, that she couldn't do anything with the child? This was a new line, when he had to come looking for her to pacify the child, and the old woman in the house, the old woman who could pacify the child by only as much as looking at it. What kind of a mug did he think she was?

Tommy did not raise his voice, nor plead, nor argue with her. He just kept on saying, 'You'd better come on home,' and calling her 'girl', and repeating that the child hadn't stopped crying for a minute since she left.

Matty coaxed and cajoled her, and at length Teasie gave in. She would only stay long enough to see to the child, not that she thought there was a happorth wrong with it, but that it was only some sort of an excuse to get her back. If it was, he should know better, because no power on earth would force her to stay in that house for another single night.

Kitty and the old woman were there when she got back. Kitty was walking backwards and forwards across the kitchen with the child, and the child was crying with all the force of its lungs. Without a word, without even taking off her still-damp coat and hat, Teasie took the child from Kitty's arms and sat down on the sofa. She saw Tommy go back into the hall, and quite suddenly she knew what he was going to do. She said nothing. Then there came the click of the big key in the lock.

Tommy came back into the kitchen. Without speaking, he sat down on the stool opposite, and began poking at the fire.

Slowly and quietly, and almost without knowing so, Teasie began to cry. The tears crept down her cheeks, and she bent her head over the child. Tommy looked over at her, his face expressionless. A thin jet of smoke came streaming from a lump of coal he had split in the fire.

Kitty dropped down on the sofa beside Teasie. She put her hand on her shoulders.

'There now,' she said, 'it'll be all right, it'll be all right.'

Teasie did not look up. No one said anything else.

There was no sound, save that of Teasie's stifled, almost inaudible sobs, and the gradually quietening gulps of the child.

9

Neilly came walking down the Asylum Hill as quickly as the heavy, well-filled shopping bag which he was carrying would allow. His right shoulder ached, and he changed his burden over to his other hand. It swung against his legs, and the big pint bottle of paraffin oil struck him squarely on the kneecap. He gave the bag another savage dunt, which only served to hurt him all the more; he scraped it roughly down along the wall to get his own back.

He was sick and fed up with this having to run up to Moore and Robinson's two or three times a week, when he got home from school. Today he had wanted to take a race out and look for shamrock with the other boys.

'Let Shemie do the messages the day,' he had cried. 'How is it it's always me who has to do them? Sure that fellow doesn't know what shamrock is. It's a dirty big bunch of clover he'll bring in.'

But Kitty, undisturbed by the probability of Shemie bringing in clover instead of shamrock, had thrust the wee note and the leather bag into Neilly's unwilling hand, and pushed him out by the scruff of the neck into the street.

Neilly gave the bag another dunt, and kept it swinging to and fro for a while as he hurried along. Ah, well; he was near back anyway; the boys would still be out. He had plenty of time yet to go and have a look for them.

The afternoon sunshine fell upon the clean dry road, and Neilly began to whistle. He hoped it would be like this tomorrow, St Patrick's Day. They were going to have a powerful time, him and all the other boys; pictures, fish and chips in Malocca's, and all. He had saved up four and ninepence; maybe his mother would put the extra threepence to it, for going the messages, and make it five shillings. His lips parted with wonder. Five shillings! How could anyone ever spend five shillings? It was impossible, all those ha'pennies, and pennies and threepenny bits. It couldn't be done; five shillings would last you for years and years. And then the bands and the processions, and the streets all decorated. He giggled, gave a series of little hops, and swung the bag round in a complete circle. Oh boy, it was going to be great, but he'd better hurry on down quick and leave this old bag in, get out and get some real shamrock. What did that Shemie fellow know about shamrock? He'd be coming back with a bagful of clover, dandelion leaves or something. Looking for shamrock was easy if you just knew where to look – the right field.

He reached the Row at last, and half-trotted down. Bursting into the house, he swung the bag up onto the counter. There was no one in the kitchen, but he could hear his mother moving about upstairs.

She shouted down: 'Who's that? Is that you, Neilly?'

'There's the bag on the counter, Mother,' he called. 'I'm away out after the boys.'

Kitty came down the stairs.

'Sit down there first, and get your breath back. They'll not take all the shamrock, I'm sure. D'you want a cut of bread?'

'Oh, Mammy, let's go now. I'm not tired, and I don't want any bread.'

Kitty put her hand out for the bag, and Neilly turned towards the door.

'What's this?'

His mother's sharp ejaculation brought him to a halt, and he turned to see her sniffing at her fingers. A sudden unaccountable dread closed like a hood over his heart.

'What?' he stammered.

Kitty lifted the bag, and Neilly saw the dark sinister stain. He felt his mouth go dry. His mother touched the stain with her fingers, and then she opened the bag and peered in.

'Sacred Heart of Jesus, this night and day!'

A fearful gush of terror swept through Neilly's brain. He stood rooted to the spot, incapable of thought or movement.

Kitty still held the bag open. Her face was slack and vacant.

'Take a look in there,' she said quietly. 'Go on! Take a good look.'

Neilly gaped dumbly into the bag, but his mind refused to register what his eyes beheld.

'You'll be killed!' Kitty screamed at him, suddenly. 'Your father will take your sacred life. Look at it! Everything in the bag destroyed with paraffin oil. What were you doing, answer me that, will you, what were you doing? How could you break a big thick pint bottle? Could you not see the oil dripping down? Could you not even smell it? Look at the floor. Look at the line of it on the floor! Were you blind, or what, that you couldn't see it coming along the road? What were you doing? Jesus, Mary and St Joseph, but I wouldn't be safer a hundred thousand miles away from about you all.'

Neilly burst into tears.

'Oh, Mammy, Mammy, Mammy, what'll I do, what'll I do?' The words rushed from him in a terror-stricken flow, a wild, desperate, terror-stricken howl.

'Shut up!' Kitty shouted. 'It's too late for crying now. Shut up, for God's sake, till I see what you've done.'

Gently and fearfully she slipped out the broken paraffin oil bottle, with the newspaper in which it was wrapped, soaked and dripping. She laid it on the floor.

'In smithereens,' she muttered dazedly. 'How did you manage to do it?' she cried again. 'That's what I'd like to know. What in under God were you doing? You must have been walking along battering it against every lamp-post you saw. Look at it, the good butter ruined. Ruined! Ruined! Ah, isn't that a terror? If that isn't a mortal sin I don't know, and some people going about that can't even afford to buy a pick of margarine.'

Kitty extracted the goods from the bag one by one, her face sickened at the piteous waste.

'Matches, cigarettes, cornflour, salt, all destroyed, not one bit of use. I might as well take them round and throw them into the Callan River. Oh, but wait, wait, you'll sup sorrow with a spoon of grief when your father hears about this. He'll kill you coul' coul' dead.' Kitty surveyed the wreckage on the counter. 'Ah now, isn't that a shame? Wouldn't that break your hearts?'

Neilly's tears rushed out afresh.

'Ah, Mammy. I didn't know. I didn't mean it. Don't tell my father, and you can take all my money, oh, and I'll kill myself, I'll kill myself –'

He stopped suddenly as the front-door latch lifted and a man came in; it was old Mick Murphy. He came in with a hop and a snitch of a song on his lips. At the sight of Kitty's face and Neilly's swollen stricken eyes, his song faded.

'Well, well, well,' he said, 'what's wrong here?'

Kitty half turned, as though she was going to walk away. Then she gestured toward the counter.

'Aye, what's wrong? Take a look at that sorrowful collection, and the paraffin oil running out of them.'

Old Mick touched one of the wrappings and sniffed at his fingers.

'Aye,' he sighed, 'troth, it's paraffin oil all right. There's a brave sup round them.'

'D'you think you could do anything at all with them, Mick? My heart's scalded. The butter's ruined, I know, but do you think you could do anything about the cigarettes? The Woodbines don't seem to be too bad – but the Players? What am I going to do with this wee fellow at all? He'll be murdered when his father comes back.'

In the comfortable and reassuring presence of old Mick, Neilly felt the agony in his heart lessen a little. He looked up hopefully, and old Mick scraped his hand over his head.

'Ah, devil the murder, sure what is he, only a child. If he never does worse, he'll do. Eh? What do you say? Eh?'

Old Mick began to finger through the stuff on the counter.

'Well, you can cancel the butter, missus. A slab of that, eh, on your bread, and you'd see stars.'

'I don't mind so much about the ould butter, Mick; I might have enough to last me over. But what about the Players?' She picked up the big carton. 'Five hundred Players!' she said bitterly. 'Ah now, quit your talking.' She turned to Neilly again. 'It's the blessing of God that your father is up the town this day.'

Old Mick took the box from her, opened it and extracted a couple of packets. He turned them over in his fingers, and sniffed at them.

'Ah, there's devil the happorth wrong with them, woman dear,' he decided. 'This ould covering over them, whatever kind of stuff it's made of, will save them all.' He peered into the carton. 'Some of them may be a wee bit damp. Stand them on the hob there for a while, and sure nobody'll be able to tell a bit of difference' He opened the Woodbine boxes. 'The ould Woods were lucky, eh? Not a drop.'

'And that's a good job for that boy,' Kitty said, 'for nothing on God's holy earth would have saved him then. I'll have to throw the salt out, Mick, and the cornflour and the matches. They're beyond recall. I don't know what to do about the butter. Maybe I could chance scraping some off a bit, and using the rest up some road. It seems a shame to throw it out.'

Neilly was trying to edge round the counter into the kitchen, but Kitty caught hold of his shoulder.

'Where are you going? You're not going in there to sit and groan. Get away out to hell's gates from about the place, for if your father comes in now, you'll be stiffened! You'll never open your cheeper again.'

'I only want to get a drink,' Neilly muttered.

'Well, give your face a rub when you're down there. You needn't go out like that; you're like a sick black.' Kitty picked up the old paraffin oil bottle, still wrapped in the sodden newspaper, and Mick and her began to examine it.

When Neilly came back up the hall, she handed it to him.

'I'll have to clear all this stuff away quick, for if that man, Mick, walked through that door now, we'd never hear the end of it. Throw that,' she said to Neilly, 'away out over the Asylum wall, as far as you can throw it. It might be as well for you to throw yourself over after it.'

As Neilly lifted the latch she said suddenly: 'And go down, you, on your knees the night, and say a prayer for Mick Murphy, for your life he has saved this day. Did you get me that snuff?'

Neilly searched in his pocket, and silently handed over the small quarter-ounce poke. Kitty took it.

'It's a wonder you didn't lash the paraffin oil round that as well,' she said.

Hiding the broken bottle as best he could behind his back, Neilly walked up the Row. There were only two old men standing at the Corner. They paid no attention to him, and he raced round to the Bridge wall, and flung the bottle, paper and all, out into the river. He craned listlessly over the Bridge, watching the circle of ripples beating out. He turned, and stood with his back against the low stone wall, staring unhappily up and down the road. He no longer felt any desire to go out for shamrock, and for a long time he stood without moving, miserable and dejected, not knowing what to do, and worrying over what would happen if his father ever found out. He had heard that, if anybody wanted anything, and if they prayed to St Anthony for it, they would get it. He cast his eyes up and prayed: 'St

Anthony, please don't let my father find out about the paraffin oil.' It seemed rather a short prayer. But he couldn't think of anything else to say, so, after a moment, be blessed himself and stood out from the wall, feeling a little better.

There was nobody about at all, and he began to dawdle slowly down the road. At the corner of the Stony Loaning he halted, wondering where the boys could have gone for the shamrock. They could have gone up the Mullinure Loaning to the railway banks, or they might have gone on down the straight road. 'Ah-h-h-h!' He turned and walked down the Stony Loaning.

As he went along, he picked up a stone now and again and hinched it over the high, unkempt hedges on either side. His spirits were beginning to lighten. Maybe his father mightn't find out after all. He stopped impulsively in the middle of the loaning, and said his prayer again, bowing his head on his chest, and clasping his hands, fingers extended beneath his chin, like he'd seen the saints and angels in the holy pictures.

When he reached the gate in Horans' field, about a hundred yards down the loaning, he stood leaning on it for a moment. Over against the far hedge, and far down the field, he could see the little shed where Johnny Kelly kept his donkey.

'This used to be a good field for shamrock,' he muttered to himself. So he stood for a while looking in and shooting out his underlip, as if he could actually see the sprigs and was sorting out the best ones to pick before he went in.

Then he climbed over and dropped down. He walked through the field with his head bowed and his hands behind his back, like an old man pondering over some grave problem. He scoured the field for over a quarter of an hour, but beyond a few miserable little stems, which he threw away in disgust, he could find nothing. Three or four times he thought he had lit on a lovely sprig, but each time his excited fingers revealed the grey, treacherous V, and he would rise up slowly, grunting 'Clover! Dirty ould clover! Shemie will have enough of that.'

Just when he was about to give up his search, he heard voices, and the sound of footsteps coming up the straight road. He recognised the voices, and ran up a bit to where he knew there was a gap. He climbed through and stood at the side of the road. The boys saw him and shouted. He stood waiting on them coming up.

'Did you get any?' he shouted. 'I was in Horanses field there, and there wasn't a pick.'

The boys waved brown paper bags at him.

'What took you in there? Why didn't you come on down? We found a great place, it's lined with it.'

Neilly took the bag from Shemie.

'Let's have a look.' He peered in, and took some out in his fingers. 'Ah, sure that's not shamrock, for God's sake.'

'What's not shamrock?' all the boys shouted. 'That's powerful shamrock. None of your old V's on that!'

Neilly smiled, and handed Shemie back his bag.

'Where did you get it?'

The boys began to direct him, all shouting together, and then they continued on slowly back towards the Row.

A little way past the end of the Asylum wall, Shemie said suddenly: 'Wait!'

The boys stopped, and looked at him.

'Let's climb up and see if there's any patients coming,' Shemie said. 'Look at what I've got.'

He took a packet of Woodbines from his pocket, and held it out in the palm of his hand.

You stole that bag, boy,' Neilly accused, quickly.

'Ah, what's stealing,' Shemie sneered. 'Maybe you never lifted anything. Oh no, the wee saint!'

'I might have lifted an ould caramel,' Neilly said, 'but I never pinched any fags.'

'Well, I only took them for a poor ould patient. You mind your own business.'

From over the wall at that moment there came the shuffling of approaching feet, faint at first, but gradually sharpening. A thin, cracked voice broke out into a song.

'There's a batch now,' one of the boys shouted, 'come on quick.'

'Ah, it's only women!'

'Well, no matter!'

The boys turned towards the wall, but Neilly caught Shemie by the shoulder and made a grab at his hand. After the ruin he had caused today, he could not bear to see Shemie deliberately throwing away more cigarettes from his mother's precious stock.

'Give us those Woodbines,' he shouted. 'D'you think I'm going to let you throw a good packet of Woodbines over to a crowd of ould patients?'

Shemie struck out with all his strength, with his free left hand, and Neilly staggered back. The younger boy leapt towards the wall and began speeling up, but Neilly sprang after him, caught him by the heels, and pulled him down. They fell on the footpath, and rolled over wrestling; with Shemie punching and kicking every chance he got. The boys crowded round excitedly, all thought of the patients forgotten. Shemie managed to scramble to his feet. His hair hung down over his eyes, and in his flushed face, his eyes glittered like beads. He held his hand up.

'I've still got it! I've still got it!' he shouted.

He ran up the footpath and then, before Neilly could grab him again, he had swung his arm, and the cigarettes went sailing over the wall. There came back a cry, as they fell amongst the passing patients.

'There's your cigarettes for you!' he panted. 'There's your cigarettes for you!' He bent down quickly and lifted up a big stone.

'If you come near me,' he cried out to Neilly, 'I'll take your head off with this stone.'

'Oh, you can drop your stone, big fellow,' Neilly sneered. 'I suppose you think you're a big fellow. If you knew what happened the day, you wouldn't have done that. But wait, wait till you go to Confession; we'll see what you'll say then.'

Shemie lowered the stone curiously.

'Why, what happened?'

Neilly turned away slowly, brushing his clothes.

'Never mind,' he said shortly, 'never mind.'

His face puzzled and curious, Shemie threw the stone away, and he and the other boys trailed slowly up after Neilly. Shemie kept looking at him.

'What happened the day, Neilly? What happened the day?'

But Neilly walked on silently, with his head averted.

Johnny Kelly's donkey and cart was in the street, but there wasn't a strand of hay on the ground for it. The door was closed, and neither Kelly nor Pachy were to be seen. Neilly hardly noticed the donkey and cart. His mind was occupied by two things only – Was his father in? If so, had he found out?

When they reached the door of their house, he hesitated, with his hand on the latch. The baker's cart passed by, with the big iron-rimmed wheels crunching noisily over the ground. Neilly's heart thudded painfully.

'Oh, if my father's in – Oh, St Anthony, please don't let my father be in.'

Shemie looked at him curiously.

'Go on in, boy. What are you standing there for?'

Neilly curled his lip and looked round at him. Then a shock of joy raced through him as, the crunch of the baker's cart fading, he caught the sound of Pachy's voice from within. Instantly he pushed the door open and burst in.

Pachy was standing in the hall, behind the counter, and over beyond, in the kitchen, were Kitty and Malachey. Malachey apparently was not long in, because he was still dressed in his good, navy-blue suit.

As Neilly entered, Pachy turned to see who it was. At the very first glance Neilly knew that he was drunk. His face was sullen, haggard and blank, and he looked at Neilly without the slightest trace of recognition in his eyes. Neilly's eager 'Hello, Pachy!' faded from his lips.

Pachy turned again towards Kitty and shrugged his shoulders, staggering a little.

'Christ the night!' he said thickly. 'St Patrick's Day! I'm only asking for a couple of shillings. You'll get it back. I tell you I'll have my Reserve money in the morning.'

'And where do you think I'll see you in the morning?' Kitty asked. 'St Patrick's Day, and you out rolling in the gutter. Oh, yes; I'd get it back, all right.'

Pachy gazed at her in silence for a moment. Then, slowly, he turned his head towards Malachey. His stomach throbbed, and a gust of sour wind rushed up his throat. He closed his lips tightly, and dug his chin in against his chest.

'Malachey –' he began, but Malachey cut him short.

'It's no use looking at me, Pachy. I'd like to have a loc of pints myself now and again, but I can't afford it. I'd look a quare fool giving you money to drink, when I can't afford it myself.'

'Oh, come on; don't give me that, Malachey. You're the ould boy has it.'

Malachey turned round towards the fire-board.

'It's all right talking. Damn the ha'penny I have more nor anyone else.'

Pachy's glazed eyes turned upon the two boys. Neilly saw the brown porter scum at the corner of his mouth. The lips puckered up in the old mocking quirk.

'Well, well, well,' he said, 'by the left, what d'you think of that? They wouldn't even lend us an ould coul' shilling. There's a fellow there would lend me a shilling if he had it.' He ran his hand over Neilly's head. 'Wouldn't you, eh?'

Neilly nodded silently, his heart overflowing with sadness and pity.

'I would, too, Pachy,' Shemie said.

'Would you now?' A glint of tears brightened the haze in Pachy's eyes.

'Come you in here, you two,' Kitty called, and the boys obeyed, crushing silently past Pachy through the red curtains.

Pachy leaned back.

'Well, you're not going to lend me a shilling, eh? Well, well, well! One mingy ould bob! Malachey,' he tightened his lips again, against the wind rising up in his throat, 'Malachey, I served in Indi' for seven years. Seven long ould years. I've roughed it, Malachey – you know that.' He lifted his head and nodded out towards the door. 'I worked in that ould Mill over there when I was sixteen years of age, six o'clock in the morning to six o'clock at night. You know that, Malachey, six o'clock in the blinking morning, but no matter now, no matter. And then one day I looked up, and I saw the dust flying round me, the ould dust, Malachey – I don't have to tell you about that. Well, one day, anyway, I looked up and I sees the dust flying round me, so I puts on the ould coat. Yes, there and then, no hesitation, I throws on the ould coat, and up to Barrack Hill. Says I, "Mister, I hear yez are looking for soldiers up here." And what d'you know, they were! As luck would have it, that's just what they did happen to be looking for that day. So in I goes. Eighteen years of age, sign on here, yes, sir.' He made a scribble in the air with his hand. 'Well, no matter, I saw it through, I served my seven, and what I don't know about Indi' – well – I seen those boyos coming creeping down out of the hills at night, big fellows . . . they could have broke you in half.'

He drew his hand over his chin.

'Big black be'rds! Christ, they'd have ate you without salt. Yes, I seen them! But no matter, fair's fair, fair's fair. I done my seven, and now I'm home here without a butt. Me and Kelly, we're all right. Kelly's over across there; he's all right – yes, I done my seven, Malachey, many a night I sat out there, and I thought about the ould Row, and I cried. Yes, I cried my bellyful, I'm not ashamed to say it. But I came through the mill, never mind, I saw it through all right, and now I'm home here without a butt. But don't worry, Malachey, don't worry, I'll have plenty of money yet. I'll have more money than anybody in this Row will ever see.'

'Well, it's nice to know that, anyway,' Kitty said, 'though how you're going to manage it, if you keep on at your present pace, is a mystery to me. If it's around me you're trying to get, Pachy, you might as well save your breath. I can put up with a lot, but you've gone too far. You might as well run on now, because if you talked from this until you were black in the face, I still wouldn't give you a ha'penny. I've tried to help you, Pachy, but you don't want anybody's help, unless it's a few shillings slipped into your hand when your Reserve money runs out. All you want to do is run about the country on Johnny Kelly's donkey and cart, have a good time, and don't let anybody worry you. Often and often I've seen me standing here, like an ould mug, handing you out money, money that I could very ill afford. But that's all over now, Pachy, I'm just beginning to catch myself on. You can run on now, run on, for you'll never get another ha'penny here, the longest day you live.'

Pachy stood with his hands in his pockets, and pursing his lips. He lifted one of the lemonade bottles from beside the scales on the counter, and held it up as though he were examining its contents curiously.

'How would you like that smashed up against the banisters?' he asked.

Kitty raised her fist.

'If you darr to break one single thing in this house, now I'm warning you, I'll get you three months in jail! You think you're a great fellow, coming in here, trying to scarr a woman, and that man standing there with a lame leg. But you won't cow me. If you don't leave that bottle down and get outside this house this minute, I'll have you lifted before night.'

'You'd better go, Pachy,' Malachey advised. 'You won't do yourself any good carrying on like that.'

Pachy stood for a moment, holding the lemonade bottle up by the neck. The boys regarded him fearfully. Then, slowly, he relaxed. The bitter, ironical smile returned to his lips.

'Well, maybe you've got something there, Malachey. Maybe you're right.' He set the bottle back again on the counter. 'You're my sister, Kitty, you're all right. No hard feelings.' Tears again glinted in his eyes. 'It's true, I'm nothing for you to feel very proud over, but no matter, you're my sister, you're all right.' He turned, lifted the latch and walked out, closing the door quietly behind him.

That night, Neilly was awakened by Eugene coming up to bed. He lay still and watched his brother undress, and crush in beneath the clothes, whistling softly and tunelessly between his teeth. Then Kitty came up and lifted the lighted candle from the chair and turned into the back room. Neilly could hear his father still moving about in the kitchen. Then in a little while, he came up as well, limping up the stairs.

The clock struck, and he counted the chimes. Eleven o'clock! In another hour it would be St Patrick's Day. No school in the morning, ha, ha, ha! He smiled happily in the dark. His father had not found out about the paraffin oil after all. Kitty had cautioned him out in the yard after teatime. 'I haven't said anything to your father, but it's not all over yet, for if anybody passes any remarks about those Players –'

Neilly knew that old Eoiny McParland, the breadman, always bought a packet of Players when he called in the morning. But just now he felt too happy and too sleepy to worry. Tomorrow was St Patrick's Day, and there was no school!

He was dropping off to sleep again when the sound of a song came floating up from the street below. It was faint at first, and he could only make out the slow, sad air. Then, as the singers grew closer, he recognised, for the second time that day, the voice of his uncle Pachy, and, joining in with him, Johnny Kelly. He lay wide awake now, listening alertly. Beside him, Shemie slept on, but across the room Eugene's bed creaked, and he could sense his brother leaning up on his elbow and listening too. He heard his mother and father whispering in the back room. The door was pulled open slightly, and the yellow candlelight gleamed out. The singing grew louder. Despite the rough, unsteady voices, the sad and lovely air, coming in through the darkness, stirred his heart strangely.

> I cursed three times since last Easter Day,
> At Mass time once I went to play,
> I passed a graveyard one day in haste,
> And forgot to pray for my mother's rest.
> I bear no hate against living thing,
> But I love my country before the King,
> So bless me, father, and let me go,
> To die if God has ordained it so.

The song stopped. Some muttering followed, and then the sound of a boot, scuffling on the door; then the sound of the door opening, and clashing shut again. A soft tide of silence rolled over everything. Neilly relaxed back upon the mattress, with Pachy's song echoing through his mind.

The silence remained unbroken and, in a little while, he fell asleep.

10

The next morning, while his father was down the hall washing, Neilly took the leather taws from the press in the little room, and hid them in his school-bag. If the breadman did say anything about the Players, well, he was making sure that he wouldn't get a belting with the taws, anyway. He remembered the last time!

He tried to keep his father in as good a humour as possible. He dressed himself quickly, without any dilly-dallying, and tried to make Shemie do likewise. He washed his face and neck scrupulously, making sure not to get too much soap caught round the backs of his ears, and then, without waiting to be told, he got some soda farls from the cupboard and sliced them straight and clean, spreading a newspaper first of all to save the tablecloth.

His eyes seldom left the clock. The breadman usually came in above nine. He dreaded the crunch of the wheels outside the door, at the same time longing with all his heart to get it over.

At ten past nine, his mother and the breadman came in together, his mother returning from eight o'clock Mass. Neilly sat watching the breadman with deathly fascination over the top of his *Comic Cuts*. This was the man who held his life in his hands.

The breadman stood talking to Malachey and Kitty. Each time he smiled, a long furrow appeared in his thin bearded cheeks. Kitty served him with his large Players, tightening her lips over at Neilly. The breadman tore off the transparent covering and, rolling it up between forefinger and thumb, tossed it over the counter into the fire. He opened the box, and offered the card out to Shemie. Then, slowly, he extracted a cigarette. He lit it. He inhaled a few times, deeply. He did not say anything, and smoked on without giving the cigarette a second glance.

Neilly let his breath out slowly, in an ecstasy of relief. Saved! Saved! His heart flooded over with happiness. He bent over Shemie's shoulder, to admire the bright, new cigarette card which his brother was holding in his hand.

After breakfast, Kitty sorted out too sprigs of shamrock, and pinned them to their jackets.

'There you are,' she said. 'Away you go, and don't roll in the muck in them good suits.'

As they walked up the Row, Neilly said: 'Come on over and see if Pachy's up.'

The boys had heard their father and mother talking about him and Kelly during breakfast.

'I suppose they're sitting over there without a bite,' Kitty had said. 'Well, if they are, that's their lookout! They'll not get me running over after them this morning.'

The boys crossed over and peered through the tears in the old curtain over the window. There was no one in the kitchen; they could see the heel of a loaf, and a tin of condensed milk on the bare table.

Neilly put his lips to the keyhole and called softly. Next moment, as though in direct answer, the patter of stockinged feet sounded faintly from up the stairs and Pachy's voice shouted, 'Who's there?' The feet descended, the key rattled in the lock, and Pachy looked out. The hair was standing on him, and his face was dark with beard stubble.

'Oh, it's you!' He smiled. 'Where in the name of God are you going to at this hour? What time is it?'

'We're going to Chapel. It's about half past nine.'

'Oh, yes; St Patrick's Day. Holiday of Obligation!'

'Where's Johnny Kelly?' Neilly asked. 'Is he in?'

'Kelly? Kelly's lying up the stairs, dead. Are you coming in to say a prayer for him?'

The boys drew back, shocked.

'Johnny Kelly, dead?'

'Aye, dead asleep.'

They smiled. 'Ah, you're only funning!'

Pachy said: 'Where's Kate? Is she in?'

'She says that if you're sitting over here without a bite it's your own lookout,' Shemie told him seriously. 'She says she's not coming over again.'

Pachy broke into a laugh.

'Did she? Well, what d'you know? Never mind, a drop of black tay'll do us rightly. It's a bad thing to be ateing all the time.'

A voice cried from upstairs: 'Who's that, Pachy?'

'God help us,' said Pachy, 'the dead has riz.'

'Ah, it's only the boys,' he called up. 'Go back to sleep again.' He nodded out towards the street. 'Who's that? Is that young Devine waiting on you over there?'

The boys turned and nodded. Neilly shouted: 'Wait there, Jackie.'

They said 'so long' to Pachy. Pachy saluted them and closed the door again. The boys crossed over to where the other lad was standing, and they strolled up to the Corner.

They stood against the Dining Room, emitting now and then a series of short, piercing whistles and, one by one, other boys came running up from their houses. They stood together for a little while making remarks, complimentary and otherwise, about each other's shamrock. When there were about eight of them, they moved away, and trotted up the road, laughing and jingling their money. They were in great spirits, for it was a lovely morning, clear and warm, with the sun already shining, and the birds singing. Halfway up the Asylum Hill they unpinned their shamrocks and 'drownded' them by dipping the sprigs into the little drain running beneath the hedge. They held them under for a good while, to make sure they were well

113

and truly 'drownded', and then, with a great deal of lip-twisting and screwing down of the eyes, they repinned their sprigs and continued on their way.

They walked about the town, after Mass was over, admiring the decorations. The place was brilliantly decked out for the great occasion. All the shops were closed, and arches and banners gaily coloured and bearing numerous inscriptions, stretched across the street. Flags hung from the windows, drooping in the warm, breezeless air. The Mass crowds dandered about slowly in their Sunday finery. Despite the crowds, the streets were comparatively quiet, but in the soft murmur of the people's voices there could be sensed an air of tense excitement and expectancy. The boys took a walk up towards Scotch Street, at the far end of the town but, just as they expected, this street was bare, colourless and empty. One or two of the boys, in a fit of bravado, shook their fists.

'You Prodesans better stay in your houses the day,' they jeered.

The sunny, lifeless street offered no taunt in return, so the boys drew back into their own domain, and hurried down towards the station to meet the bands coming off.

The first train had come in, and the first band had already formed up. It was coming through the station gates when the boys drew near. They raced down the few remaining yards, and crushed in towards the crowds, their hearts hammering, at the sight of the great resplendent banner which was being carried along in front of the band. It was a flute band, and the sweet, piercing music of the flutes flowed out joyfully, stabbing like little silver lances into the hearts of the people.

Three more bands followed, two pipe and one melodeon. The crowd cheered and clapped, their heads growing light with the music and the colour, and the great splendid flowing banners, in which were portrayed some of the more glorious and soul-stirring episodes from the history of Ireland. St Patrick banishing the snakes, pointing sternly downwards. Mass in the Papal Days! The priest crouching before the altar in the little dark cave; behind him the white, exalted faces of the worshippers, and then far, far out over the hills, two evil priest-hunters, one pointing and grimacing with satanic joy, the other aiming his rifle – the Battle of the Yellow Ford; the Siege of Limerick; the Battle of the Boyne; Brian Boru at Clontarf. The vivid wondrous banners, with their long golden tassels, cast a spell over Neilly and his friends. Their eyes devoured the front picture, as each band came up, and then, as it passed, they jumped up wildly to see what was on the other side.

The fourth band passed, and most of the crowd went off behind it. The music seemed to have driven young Devlin, the Preacher, temporarily insane. He stalked up and down, his eyes glittering, shouting out threats of what would happen if everybody didn't get out of town. People were looking at him curiously, and smiling. Neilly gave him a push and shouted for him to stop.

Another train had come in; there would be more bands; but the boys decided to rush on home quickly and get their dinner, and then come right back again. Any bands which they missed they could easily see up the town.

They got back about two o'clock and were astonished to see how much the crowds had swollen. The streets were black, and it was as much as they could do to crush along the footpath against the walls of the shops. The public houses were doing great trade, and every one they passed had an especially thick knot of men crowded round outside, sipping at their big black pints, hats tilted back from their sweat-pricked foreheads. Now and again the skirl of the pipes, or the lilting berl of the melodeons, struck upon the boys' ears, and they would all crush desperately over to the edge of the footpath to watch the band hammer briskly by.

There was a big demonstration in the athletic grounds at three o'clock, and the bands were making in that direction. The boys decided, however, to go to the pictures. As they sat in the hot darkness, watching the cowboys careering across the screens, now and again, between the crash of the gunshots and the thunder of the hoofs, they could hear the music outside, the sweet, sunny music of the flutes, punctuated sometimes by the wild, tipsy shout of a drunk.

The matinee finished at five o'clock, and the boys came out into the sun, dazzled and holding up their hands. They made their way up into the main street; it was a moving river of people, and the boys hesitated on its edge, wondering if they would ever be able to get through.

Someone shouted: 'Look, Neilly, there's Eugene. Eugene! Hi! Eugene!'

Neilly squinted under his hand, and saw Eugene stop and look over. He was wheeling his bicycle, one hand on the handlebars, the other on the saddle.

'Are you not riding, Eugene?' Neilly asked, when at length he managed to get over to him.

'What?' said Eugene, 'in this crowd? You'd never get through them. Where were you all? Does my mother know you're up here? You'll be crushed to death.'

'Ah, we'll not be crushed, we were at the pictures there. Tom Mix, boy, powerful!'

'Where are you going to now?'

'Down to Malocca's for a feed, then we're all going back to the pictures again.'

The crowd was forcing them apart.

'You'd be as well to go on down home out of this,' Eugene called. 'This is no place for you to be hanging about. Did you see my father or anybody?'

Neilly shook his head vigorously. Shemie shouted: 'Give us a ride, Eugene.' 'I can't. How can I?' Eugene waved his hand. 'Go on home. Be seeing you.'

'I'm not going to go home,' somebody said.

'I'm going down to Malocca's for fish and chips.'

'Malocca's'll be packed!'

'I don't care. I'm going down, anyway.'

'Come on, and we'll all go down.'

Outside Malocca's, the crowd was even worse than they had anticipated. The people were clustered black around the door, and the aisle down between the snugs was thronged. The boys gallantly flung themselves into the fray.

In about a quarter of an hour they emerged again onto the footpaths, carrying four penny, brown paper pokes of chips. They ate the hot, salty potato chips, standing up against the window, and then, consumed with thirst, Neilly and another lad detailed themselves off to crush in again and try to get some lemonade. In ten minutes they were out once more, battered, trampled on, growled at, but smiling. Each had his arms lapped tightly around four lemonade bottles.

'Did you get them opened?' someone cried.

The faces of the two boys fell, their triumph turning to ashes.

'Surely you couldn't have forgot to get them opened. How'll we drink them now? You'll have to go back with them.'

Neilly looked at the crowd in dismay.

'You'd never get in there again. Has anybody got a knife? Vincent, you've got a knife, where is it?'

The penknife was handed over, and Neilly opened it and dug the point of the blade under the tin cap of one of the bottles.

'Ah, open mine, Neilly,' Shemie cried. 'I'm dry.'

'For God's sake, wait there,' said Neilly.

He worked the blade up and down, and a slight fizz became audible; he prized harder, and the lid suddenly popped off, and the creamy foam gushed out. Like a flash Neilly closed his lips over the bottle, rolling his eyes in delight, at the lemonade's sharp delicious bite.

They stood there drinking, oblivious to everything but the gratification of their thirst.

Three big girls passed, linking one another. One of them smiled over at Neilly.

'There's a lovely wee fellow. I wonder if he'd coort.'

Neilly, who had had the bottle tilted up, blushed a deep red, and nearly choked himself. He burst into a fit of coughing, and the girls walked on laughing.

When they had finished, they saw by a clock in a window opposite that it was a quarter past six. Just at that moment, as though in confirmation, the cathedral clock struck ding dong, ding dong, the soft golden notes creeping down to them through the noise of the street.

'Come in!' said Neilly. 'We'd better get going. The first house starts at a quarter to seven.'

'Seven!' someone objected.

'I'm telling you, a quarter to seven. Six forty-five. What class are you in, infants?'

'Well, there's plenty of time, even so.'

'How is there plenty of time? D'you know what kind of a crowd'll be up there? How is there plenty of time?'

As they were coming up in the middle of the crowd, towards the junction of Russell Street, they suddenly heard a great deal of shouting and cursing going on. All around them men started running forward, and in a moment a large bunch had gathered at the head of the street.

'It's a fight!' the boys shouted. 'Come on.'

They rushed over excitedly, and wormed their way in. When they got to the forefront, Neilly's heart jumped with terror. It was Pachy and Johnny Kelly, and they were fighting with three big black-haired fellows, with green sashes over their shoulders. Pachy knocked one of the big fellows spinning, and, as he floundered back,

Pachy gripped the sash and tore it from him in one great chuck.

All five of them seemed to be mad drunk. One swung an empty bottle at Johnny Kelly's head. He missed, and went staggering against the crowd, only to be spurned relentlessly back into the arena again. The crowd cheered and hooted, but no one made the slightest attempt to stop the fight. Pachy's argument for some reason seemed more against the bright green sashes than with the men themselves, for every time he got the chance he would make a grab at one of the two remaining ones, and give it a wrench.

At length he did manage to pull another one off. Then somebody shouted: 'Police!' The crowd broke. A big, red-faced policeman came rushing through. He charged at Pachy, baton upraised. Neilly screamed. The baton came down on Pachy's head, and his knees buckled. As he slumped, he flung his arms out and caught the big policeman around the neck. Neilly saw him shake his head, and, blinded with pain, drag himself up again, clawing onto the policeman. As he came up, he swung his head and crashed it, with all his remaining strength, against the policeman's face. Both of them fell to the ground.

Two more policemen broke through the crowd, batons ready for action. Kelly faced them, swinging his fists wildly, but a baton thumped against his shoulder, and he went down too. Making no attempt at resistance, the other three fellows held up their hands.

'They started the fight,' one of them kept shouting, in a broad up-the-country voice. 'They started the fight, that fellow there!' He pointed to Pachy. 'He said that these were Orangemen's sashes. That's the fellow. We're not to blame. That's your man!'

Pachy and Kelly were hauled to their feet. The big policeman rose up, too, and began brushing his trousers down in a bewildered fashion. Someone handed him his cap and baton, and he took them dazedly. Blood running from his nose streaked his face and tunic. He staggered forward and put his hand on Pachy's shoulder. Pachy looked at him. Neither of them said anything.

The five of them were marched down Russell Street, towards the police barracks. The big Free State fellow kept on shouting: 'You can't lift us! That fellow started it. There's your man there – you black, Northern bastard.'

One of the policemen gave his shoulder a shake, and he became silent.

The crowd began to follow, but they were gestured back. Neilly, who, up till now, had stood with the other boys petrified with terror, suddenly burst into tears and rushed forward. He caught his uncle by the hand.

'Pachy! Pachy!' he shouted.

One of the policemen pushed him back, and Pachy growled: 'Let him alone, you! Go on home, son,' he muttered. 'Go on home. Don't tell your mother.'

Kelly turned round too. Both their faces were white and dull with agony.

Neilly dropped back and rubbed his sleeve over his tear-filled eyes, suddenly ashamed of himself, and all the boys looking on. Shemie started to cry too.

'Quit your whingeing,' Neilly shouted at him in a rage. 'What are you blerting about?'

Out in the crowd on the main street, he suddenly caught a glimpse of Eugene again. There was another telegram boy with him. Both of them were leaning on their bicycles, looking about curiously. Apparently they had just come on the scene. They did not see Neilly or the boys till they all came rushing over.

'What! Are you still here?' Eugene ejaculated. 'What's happened? What's he crying for?'

'A policeman hit my uncle Pachy over the head with a baton,' Shemie wept. His face twisted suddenly with fury, and he turned round again in the direction of Russell Street.

'If I had a big stone,' he screamed, 'he wouldn't have hit him. I'd a cut the bloody big skull off him, so I would!'

In spite of the sudden shock, Eugene had to smile.

'Where is Pachy?' he cried. 'Is he lifted? Was Kelly there too? Did you ever see such two madmen? I'd better run down and tell my father and Tommy. I seen them at the Shambles a minute ago. Are you coming down with us, Joe?'

They swung their legs over their machines. 'Come on, never mind the crowd; ride over them.' Eugene screwed round on the saddle. 'Go on you home, Neilly, now,' he called, 'and the lot of you. Go on!'

After what had happened, none of the boys had any desire for any more pictures. They squeezed through the crowd and, about two hundred yards down, they met Malachey Coyle, Tommy and three other fellows from the Row hurrying up. Eugene and the other boy walked along with them, wheeling their bicycles.

'What happened?' Malachey questioned. Neilly caught the sweet, jammy porter smell on his breath. 'Did you see what happened?'

Neilly briefly described the fight and the arrest, and the fellows looked at one another. 'Well, they've done it this time,' Tommy said. 'They'll never get out. They'll have be'rds on them.'

'Let's take a walk up, anyway, and see if we can see them,' Malachey sighed. 'Pachy got his Reserve money the day. I knew something like this would happen. Away you on home, you two, as quick as you can get, and don't say anything to your mother till we get back.'

The boys trailed away. The cathedral clock struck seven.

The sun was still shining, but it's light was tired and stale, and the flags and arches, which that morning had looked so bright, now drooped down grey and bedraggled. They boys had no further interest in them or in the crowd. Had a band passed by, they would scarcely have noticed it.

For them, for this year, St Patrick's Day was over. They only wanted to get home.

Part II

11

The June sun shone down brightly on the Loughall Road, and the thick green hedges and the fields stretching beyond, gleamed with the brightness of new paint. Three women came in sight around a corner of the road, walking up towards the Row.

They were Kitty, Teasie and an old neighbour woman, Rosie Toal. Kitty and Teasie were wheeling prams. These were filled with sticks for the fire – dry, rotten hawthorn roots. Old Rosie carried her load on her back, held together by a well-worn rope. Although she was very much older than either Kitty or Teasie, she did not seem to feel the weight, only now and then giving the sticks a hunch up a bit with her shoulders. They had had a good gather. They walked along slowly, their eyes wrinkled up in the strong sunlight, enjoying the prospect of the bright blue sky, the green hedges, and the silence of the dusty road.

Almost three months had passed since the arrest of Pachy and Johnny Kelly. Each of them had been given three months in jail; Pachy, as the cause of the disturbance, had escaped a stiffer sentence only by reason of his not having been very long out of the army, and his good record as a soldier.

Kelly had sent word that Teasie could have the house if she wanted it. There was some talk that Pachy and he were going to pack up and clear out when their three months were up. The house would have been relet in any case, because the owners would hardly have agreed to it being held vacant, even if the rent had been collected each week – as it would have been, for Pachy and Kelly were well liked in spite of their wildness – on account of the number of names that were down for the 'next house'. The houses in the Row, despite their susceptibility to floods, were held desirable, on account of their cheapness and nearness to the Mill. Teasie, who had had her name down for a long time, heard Kelly's offer joyfully, and without any disturbance of her conscience.

'Now's your chance,' Kitty had told her, 'if you don't grab quick, somebody else will.'

Tommy, however, had not welcomed the idea very much. But Kitty had talked and argued him round to it. Quieter since the last big row, the old woman had not said very much about it, one way or the other. So Tommy and Teasie had flitted, and Neilly was sent over to live with his granny to keep her company.

There had been a lot of cleaning and patching up for Teasie to do, before she could move in, but she had entered into the work with annihilating energy. Kitty had given her a hand, and they had scrubbed the place from top to bottom, whitewashed the ceilings, the back yard, and repapered the walls. They were delighted to see that all the old jam pots, bottles and rags, which Kelly had collected in the back yard, had been disposed of. Pachy and he must have got rid of the lot the day before their arrest, for the few extra shillings.

The changeover was the best thing that could have happened to Teasie and Tommy. Away from the old woman, they got on far better, though, even yet, there were times when Tommy did not seem too happy. He would often mention to Teasie that he thought the old woman was fretting.

One last, sharp engagement had taken place, a week or so after the flitting. The old woman, sceptical as always of getting his proper food, used to call him over sometimes to her house – without anybody noticing as she thought – for a plate of potatoes and brown gravy with Neilly, and odd cups of tea. Tommy had gone, not through any slight on Teasie, or because he was hungry or anything like that, but because of the strong ties which bound him to his mother. He found them very hard to break. Of course, when Teasie found out, there was murder. Tommy said that, in future, not only would he have an odd dinner in the old woman's but he would have every meal there, breakfast, dinner and supper, and she could do whatever the hell she liked about it.

Teasie passed no more remarks, but just got his meals ready as usual. He sat down and took them and, strangely enough, there was no more heard about the old woman's potatoes and brown gravy, although he made no secret of the fact that he still dropped in now and again for a cup of tea. But Teasie was quite satisfied with her victory; the tea part she did not mind.

Teasie by no means turned her back on the old woman now that she was independent of her. She would often take a run over in the evenings and sit with her by the fire. The old woman was very fond of the child and would take him and sit jigging him up and down on her knee, chanting some of her old, old songs. Sometimes, as she sat there, Teasie would look at her and sigh. Fretting or not, there was no doubt that the old woman had failed a bit. Teasie would often make an attempt to speak to her about it. Some word of reassurance, not to worry, that Tommy was doing the best. Only she would keep silent, realising, all the time, that there was, after all, nothing that she could say. Even if she were to speak, it would do no good at all.

Neilly, however, settled down quite happily with his granny. She lavished on him most of the love and attention which she could not now give to Tommy. She cleaned his boots for him every night, and gave him a mug of milk and a big white-top before he went to bed. When Neilly told Shemie about this, Shemie broke into tears and wanted to come over and live with his granny too. Kitty gave him a warm ear, but each night from then on he was invited over too.

There was still no word of the Mill going on again!

As the three women walked along, the silence of the afternoon seemed to be intensified by the sound of the pram wheels and the screek of old Rosie's bundle. Then, from further up the road, shouts began to float down to them.

'There's a score coming down,' said Kitty. 'Better get onto the footpath there.'

They crossed onto the footpath and came up a bit further. Suddenly, and without warning, the black iron bullet came slicing around the corner making straight for them. They stopped with little ejaculations, and crushed up into the hedge, not knowing which way to turn. The bullet smacked off the cribben and rattled on down the road.

A young fellow came running round the corner, and Kitty shouted, half laughing, half-angry: 'The devil take you and that ould bullet! Somebody's leg'll be broke down this road yet.'

The young marker waved to them, smiling.

'They must be practising for the big score that's coming off,' Kitty murmured. 'Macklin's throwing some big fellow on Sunday. What's his name, the Hammer-man or something.'

As the score went past, Tommy stopped by them for a minute.

'The child's over in the ould doll's, Teasie,' he said. 'Throw a loc of them roots in for her, will you? Dambut here, you got the right bundle – what'll the old farmers burn?'

'It's a wonder you wouldn't take a race out some day yourself,' Kitty said. 'It doesn't run coal now, you know. I believe you like a hate as well as anybody.'

'Aye, now you're talking, Kate,' Tommy laughed back. 'Wouldn't I look an ornament walking down the road with a pram' – he stuttered a little – 'Lord bless us, all the cows in the country'd be after me. What!'

'H'm! That fellow won't do much,' Teasie said, as they passed on. 'He'll sit at the fire till the dead lice drop off him, but don't ask him to move.'

'Ah, now isn't it the blessing of God that it isn't wintertime,' old

Rosie remarked. 'You don't burn much in this weather, thanks be to God. A loc of ould sticks does you rightly.'

As they were coming past the Bridge wall, Kitty, looking up, noticed a woman crossing over at the bottom of the Asylum Hill. Her walk was not the walk of any Row woman, and Kitty eyed her curiously. Suddenly she recognised her as a woman from the far end of the town, with whom she had wrought for years in the Mill.

'Isn't that Ellen McGreevy of Castle Street?' she murmured. 'I wonder what she can be doing away down here? Is that yourself, Ellen?' she called out. 'God, you're far afield the day.'

The woman had been walking quickly along, her head bent as though deep in thought. Now she looked up and waved her hand.

'Oh, hello, Kitty, there you are! You're the very one I want to see.' She came over, and they all stopped at the Corner. 'Hello, Teasie, and Mrs Toal, how are you all keeping at all? Have you been out gathering sticks? Isn't that a beautiful day, thank God for it?'

Teasie and the other woman returned her greeting. Kitty looked at her with a sudden sense of foreboding.

'I just thought I'd take a wee race down and see you, Kitty, in case you'd be worried,' the woman said. 'Noel's all right now, there's not a happorth wrong with him. It'll just teach him a good lesson. He' – she broke off, as she saw Kitty's uncomprehending look – 'hasn't Eugene told you about the accident?' she queried.

A hand seemed to close over Kitty's heart.

'Well, I haven't seen him since he was down for his dinner. When did he have the accident? What happened?'

'No don't get yourself upset,' the woman soothed. 'I suppose he was afraid to say anything about it. You know what those young fellows are like.'

'Well, what happened, what happened? Was there anybody hurt? Noel! That's your wee fellow, isn't it? Oh my, oh my, will I ever get any peace on this earth? That Eugene fellow! I knew something was bound to happen the way he goes racing about on that bicycle. I've warned him as often as I've fingers and toes. Time and time again. Tsk, tsk, tsk!'

'When did this happen, Mrs McGreevy?' Teasie asked. 'This morning?'

'Sometime this morning, daughter. The first I knew of it was when I was sent down for from the infirmary. Now, now, don't get yourself all upset, Kitty, for God's sake. Noel's all right now, he's all right. He's back up in the house there, now, all right. He only got a few stitches in. Now he's all right, it'll do him all the good in the world; he was lost for something like it.'

'Wait till that Eugene fellow comes home,' Kitty said, 'I'll make his father give him the best bateing he ever got in his life.'

'Och, for God's sake away out of that,' Teasie protested. 'Sure he's only a child. What happened, anyway, Mrs McGreevy?'

'Indeed now, daughter, I don't know much about it myself. Eugene it seems had three young fellows on his bicycle –'

'Three of them on his bicycle?' Kitty ejaculated. 'God look down on us!'

'Ah, give your head peace, woman dear,' Teasie said. 'Whereabouts was this, missus?'

'Out the road somewhere. I'm not sure where. But now I'm not blaming Eugene at all. They should have let the young fellow go on about his business. That Noel! He's up to all the devilment he can put his hands on.'

Kitty sighed.

'Was there anyone else hurt, Ellen?' She put her hand on her heart. 'I'm not worth tuppence.'

'No one else was touched, Kitty, as far as I know. Now there's no call to worry. It'll be all right.'

'Come on down, Ellen, and I'll make you a cup of tay. I'm sure you could be doing with it. Come on, on down out of that, sure it's no use standing here, the whole Row'll be out. What hurry are you in? Well,' she added bitterly, 'there's the post office and all about it for you. A good job, and a good pension at the end of it. No matter how much you try with something like this. God knows what time he'll be back at the night either. He said he was going to the first house of the pictures, and that he wouldn't be home for any tay. That's the first time he ever missed his tay – I might have known that something was wrong. If he loses that good job, after all the trouble we had getting him into it, he need never set foot inside that door again. His father'll strangle him.'

As they walked down the Row, other women leaned out over their half-doors, and called out greetings to Mrs McGreevy. They watched the four women walking down, frowning, their eyes narrowed with curiosity, staring.

Tommy was sitting on the sofa, talking to Malachey and Kitty, when Eugene came in about ten o'clock. Teasie had sent him over to see that Eugene's father would not be too hard on him.

Eugene came in, whistling nonchalantly, pushing his bicycle in through the curtains. His eyes looked out alertly. He sensed that something was wrong. No one spoke. He greeted Tommy and pushed his bicycle on down the hall, into the yard.

'Pictures, Eugene?' Tommy inquired, when he came back into the kitchen.

'Aye, I went to the cinema.' He glanced quickly at his father and mother.

Malachey was sitting on the chair, elbows on his knees, holding the poker in between the two middle bars of the grate. Kitty glanced up from the sofa.

'Why didn't you tell me, boy, about the accident you had this morning?'

'What accident?' asked Eugene. The words were out of his mouth without his thinking; a desperate, half-instinctive rejection of the fact.

Malachey jumped up, the poker rattling onto the floor. He made a swipe at Eugene, his face suffused with blood, but Tommy caught him by the arm and forced him back into the chair.

'Now sit there, man dear, and rest yourself; you'll be taking a wake turn, jumping up and down like that. Eugene, for God Almighty's sake tell us the truth, will you? It'll not do you any good trying to act the innocent.'

'That wee fellow there,' said Kitty. 'He'd tell a lie would hand you at the hour of midnight.'

Eugene took his cap off. A bright wing of hair slipped over his forehead. He hooked it back sullenly with his thumb.

'Well, I couldn't help it!' Kitty cried. 'Hell, well you could help it. It wasn't for want of warning. I'm sick, sore, and tired telling you to go easy on that cursed ould bicycle. You couldn't help it! There's a young fellow lying up in the infirmary, split. You couldn't help that, I suppose?'

'He's out of the infirmary now,' Eugene said.

'Don't answer me back, or I'll stiffen you,' Kitty shouted. 'You good-for-nothing-looking craythur!'

Eugene juked back again.

'A lot you seem to care where he is! You're running to the pictures. I suppose you hardly thought it worth your while to call up and see how the young fellow was?'

'I did call up. I'm just left it, sure.'

'You're just left it, sure! I'm telling you, my boy, you're in for a quare cooling. If you lose that job up in the post office, you need never come back into this house again.'

'What the hell were you dong, anyway, or what were you thinking of?' Malachey cried. 'Why didn't you go on and deliver your telegrams? Who are you looking at, who do you think you're looking at?' He tried to rise up again, but Tommy pressed him back.

'For God's sake sit there and don't be shouting. You'll have the whole Row in.'

'I'm not looking, I'm not looking at anybody,' Eugene stammered fearfully, almost in tears. 'You're all onto me.'

'We're not onto you half enough,' his mother shot back. 'That's what's wrong with you. You've had far too easy a time. A good battering now and again would have done you all the good in the world.'

'Many a battering I've got,' Eugene sniffed.

'You'll get another one, this minute, if you're not very careful who you're talking to.'

'How did you manage to get three on the bicycle anyway?' Malachey demanded. 'That's what I'd like to know. Hell's curse, you wouldn't see the like of it in Duffy's Circus.'

'And yourself four!' Tommy took it up, trying to make a joke of it. 'Four on the one bike! Duffy's Circus would pay ten pound a week for that trick. What? Here, did you do it? Malachey and me have been sitting here all day trying to puzzle it out. You could get one on the bar, and yourself on the seat, is two. We got that far. Maybe you could manage to get another on the back mudguard somewhere. That's three. But where did you put the other one? That's the part we can't figure out, unless you stuck him into that wee pouch along of the telegrams.'

Eugene smiled tentatively.

'I put him on the handlebars,' he said.

'You put him on the handlebars!' Malachey exploded. 'Ah, now, that's enough, that's settled it. I don't want to hear any more. That'll be all!'

'Well here, tell us this, Eugene. Why? What was the idea? Were you just trying to see how many you could get on, or what? Why didn't you hang on for a while, and a couple more might have come along?'

'No, it was like this,' said Eugene, breathing a little easier. – Good man, Tommy! I'd have been wrecked if Tommy hadn't been here! – 'You know Drummond Loaning out the Moy Road, don't you? You know that bridge up at the head of the hill? Well, I was going up the hill there, and I met your three men on the top. They said they were going out to some house, somewhere –'

'So you thought you'd give them a lift! And what happened? Did you crash?'

'What else could have happened,' Malachey snarled, 'with four on the one bike? How could he miss but crash?'

'There must have been a candle lit for you somewhere,' Kitty said. 'That's all I can say. It was the blessing of God you didn't all get your necks broke.'

'And what happened then?' Tommy pressed. 'Was young McGreevy the only one hurt? What about the other two?'

'Well, young McGreevy got the worst of it. You see, he was the one who was on the handlebars. He went right over. My God, he didn't half hit the ground a thump.'

'Was he knocked out?'

'He sure was! He lay there with the blood pishing out of him. The other two boys were all right. They only got a couple of scratches. They went into the ditch, you see, on the grass.'

'And what about yourself?'

'Oh, I was all right. I got a belt on the elbow, that was all.'

'Show us that elbow,' Kitty ordered.

Eugene pulled up his right sleeve. The skin was all scraped off. 'It's all right,' he said.

'Take that coat out o' that. How is it all right? If you get a dose of blood poisoning, you'll wonder where you spent your summer. Why didn't you get some iodine or something on it?' Kitty poured some hot water into a basin and began to bathe the arm.

'Well, and what happened then?' Malachey grunted.

Eugene kept looking at his arm. The blood-tinted cloth, as Kitty dipped it in, turned the water a slight greeny colour.

'Well, I carried –'

The latch clicked and everyone's head jerked round.

'Hush,' said Kitty. 'Wait till they go out again.'

But it was only Teasie bringing Shemie back over from the old woman's. She smiled at Eugene as she came in.

'Well, are you back? I see you got a knock as well. Ah! But that's sore-looking so it is.'

Shemie screwed his mouth up.

'Oh, Eugene, look at your arm. How do you bear that? Did you fall off the bicycle?'

'Aye, he did indeed fall off the bicycle. Between him falling off the bicycle and you falling into the Callan River, I have the times of it.'

Teasie laughed.

'I haven't said anything to the ould doll. She'd be over like I don't know what, if she knew. You'd never be able to ride a bicycle again as long as you lived, Eugene.'

'Lord God, don't tell that woman,' Tommy said. 'We'd never hear the last of it.'

'Well, what then?' Kitty grunted to Eugene. 'Go on ahead. We might as well hear the remainder.'

'Well, I carried young McGreevy up to a house,' Eugene continued, 'and the man sent the other two boys down on to the main road to stop a car.'

'And did they?'

'Aye! Some ould fellow came up. He took the three of them, and he wanted me to come too, but I had to take the bike in. The ould fellow said he'd have to report the accident to the police.'

'Hell roast him,' said Kitty, 'he had little to do. Could he not have left them in and went on about his business?'

'They have to report it, Kitty, to keep themselves clear,' Tommy explained. 'Did you see the police then, Eugene?'

'Aye! One of them came down to see me.'

'Who was it, d'you know?' Malachey asked.

'Pearse, I think. Tall thin fellow, with a long nose.'

'Oh, he's a bad villain, that fellow,' Kitty said. 'That's the fellow who got young Cartmill fined for no brakes. What did he say?'

'Oh, he just asked me what happened.'

Kitty went into the room and began rummaging about in the drawers. 'I seen some bandages about here somewhere. God knows where I'm going to find them now. This is the house of the hidden mystery. You can find everything till you start looking for it.'

'Well here, Eugene,' said Tommy, 'I bet the ould bike was a bit of a mess, eh? Dambut!' he chuckled, 'you've had the right day of it. I suppose you took a run up to the pictures to get your head shired. I don't mind telling you that it's more than I could have done. What do you say, Malachey? I don't think I could have looked much at the pictures after a thing like that.'

'You needn't pass any remarks on anything that man ever does now,' Malachey grunted. 'The next time Duffys' Circus comes here, I'll take you up and get you a job in no time at all.'

Kitty came out of the room with a roll of bandage and some iodine. She began to prod Eugene's arm with the iodine cork, and Shemie twisted his lips up again.

'Oh, Eugene,' he repeated, 'how do you stick that?'

'You should have been in bed hours ago,' Kitty told him. 'Look at the time! I suppose you'll be wanting your tay now, she said to Eugene. 'Well, you'll just have to wait till it's ready. The next time you want to gallivant off to the City Cinema, come down here first ' for your meals.'

Tommy glanced up at the clock.

'What time is it, anyway?'

Eugene rolled his eyes at Teasie, and she winked back.

'You stay where you are,' she said to Tommy, 'I've got a few things I want to do first, without you tripping over me. Sure it's early yet.'

Tommy caught on too, and smiled at Eugene.

'Duffy's Circus!' he said.

12

It was very hot in the shop. The fire had been allowed to go out, and over the lower part of the window a double sheet of brown paper was pinned, to protect the sweets from the fierce glare beating through the panes. Through the paper the shadowed outlines of three flies were visible, buzzing against the glass. The front door was open, the street outside lying silent and empty in the sun.

Kitty cut the round print of butter exactly in half; the knife sliced through as though it were red-hot.

'This heat would destroy all the butter in creation,' Kitty commented, as she wrapped one of the halves and pushed it towards an old woman waiting behind the counter.

'God love you, daughter. I'll not forget you for this; I'll give you something off for sure on Friday. Tsk, tsk, tsk! D'you think the ould Mill will ever go on again? We didn't know how well off we were. Ah now, that's the way, that's the way. Well, thanks very much, Mrs Coyle.' Shaking her head dolefully, the old woman departed.

Kitty sighed, and flicked the pages of the blue jotter, which contained the accounts of all her customers. She came to the name of the old woman who had just left, and stabbed her pencil slowly up the list, her lips working. 5/9½, no 5/10½! She sighed again, and added '½ butter 6/d.'

She thumbed through the pages. Bills, bills, bills! Of course, it had always been the same, even when the Mill was on, but then they were always brave and certain of being squared up at the end of the week, But they couldn't be so sure now! Mrs Sheridan – 6/3! There's one's been lying for three weeks. They seemed to think that all she had to do was to stand behind the counter, and hand the stuff out, one thing after another. Still, what could she do? Times were hard! The ould Bureau wasn't much. It was hardly the people's fault. She didn't have the heart to refuse them a pick of butter, or an odd packet of Woodbines, now and again. After all, they had been decent enough when the money was coming in. She sighed again and closed the jotter. Taking the remaining half-pound of butter, she placed it in the basin of water in the corner of the room, where she always kept her butter in the warm weather.

She came back into the kitchen and peeped out across the street, through the upper part of the window. No sign of the priest coming out of the ould doll's yet! This was one of wee Father Toner's periodical visits to the Row. It was a brave while since he had been round before, but no one ever knew when the notion might strike him. He was a great favourite with the old woman, and he always stopped longer with her than with anyone else.

A young girl, nibbling at a large cut of bread and jam, came in for a halfpenny bar of treacle toffee. As Kitty went to the window she heard voices, and a scrape of feet, outside at the door. Tommy, Malachey and Jim Macklin, the bullet-thrower, came in.

Tommy stopped at the sight of the little girl.

'My God, the night!' he said, 'how did you get such a terrible cut in your hand? Dear, dear, that's shocking! That's young Creegan's, isn't it?' he added, when the child had left. 'That's the first time I ever seen one of them young Creegans with a cut of bread with either jam or butter on it. Somebody must have took pity on her. They say that Maggie puts all her butter into a glass jar and, when any of the youngsters come in for a piece of bread, she just gives the ould jar a roll over it and away the kid goes.'

'Away out of that,' Kitty said.

'That's the God's truth,' Tommy laughed. 'I heard that yesterday up at the Corner. Well, it's one way to save butter, eh? Sure, what

would the child know whether there was butter on its bread or not?'
He moved his hands in a rolling action. 'What!'

Macklin threw twopence on the counter.

'Give us a Woodbine, Kitty, will you, and don't heed anything
that man tells you.'

Kitty smiled as she handed him the slim, red packet.

'Go easy on the cigarettes, Jim. You'll need all your puff on
Sunday.'

'For God's sake hold your tongue, woman dear,' Tommy said.
'The Hammer-man will be so far behind that we'll be out looking for
him with flash-lamps.'

'Were you up signing on?' Kitty asked.

'Up signing on, Kitty!' Macklin answered, shaking his match to
extinguish it. 'Thon's a shocking place got altogether. Talking about
crowds! We seen young Eugene over at the post office.'

'Well?'

'We just take a walk up the yard, to see if we could see him up
in that wee room they've got up there.' Tommy had taken up the tale.

'It's a wonder you weren't threw out. Were you there, Malachey?'

Malachey had come on round into the kitchen.

'No! I wasn't up the town, sure.'

'Here, he's a shocking man that Eugene fellow,' Tommy went
on. 'What? There the two of them were sitting, him and some other
young fellow, and we could hardly get him into the place for forms
and papers, and the ink flying about. Then that wee bell started
to ring, but did anybody pass any remark? Tut, man, sense about
you! I said, "There's the bell ringing for telegrams." "Ah, let it ring
there," says Eugene. "I'm fed up listening to it. It never starts to ring
till you're doing something." "It's not our turn, anyway," says the
other fellow, "Lavery should be here, it's his turn. He's out joking
somewhere, I suppose." Lord God, I had to laugh, and Eugene sitting
there filling in reports and dispatches and one thing and another, and

the sweat blinding him. Two shocking men altogether! We left them there and came away on down home from about them.'

'He's not getting summonsed over it sure, Kitty, is he?' Macklin asked.

'No, that's one good job,' Kitty replied, 'though he has only Mrs McGreevy to thank for that. That woman is one of the very best I must say! Her young fellow lying in bed split open, and still and all, she went up to the police and barged a batter in case they were going to summons Eugene over it. "Leave the poor young fellow alone," says she. "Is he not in enough trouble already? You'll get him the sack. Sure it's none of your childer that's been hurt!" I'm telling you, it's not every day in the week that you meet a woman like Ellen McGreevy.'

Suddenly she started as, through the window, she caught a glimpse of the black figure of the priest coming over across the street, wheeling his bicycle.

'Here's Father Toner,' she whispered urgently. 'He's just been over in the ould doll's.'

Malachey jumped up quickly from the sofa.

The priest came in smiling slowly, a small dark man, with black, glowing eyes, and the hair growing grey around his ears.

'Good day, Mrs Coyle. Is that you, Malachey? How are you keeping at all? And this is Tommy here, how are you, Tommy, and' – he laughed – 'ah yes, Macklin, the bullet-thrower.'

They all returned his greeting.

'Isn't it a beautiful day?' he said.

'It's terrible warm, Father,' Kitty sighed.

'It's too warm, it is. It's nearly too warm. Ah, now; sure there's no pleasing us at all. It's one of the great faults of human nature that we're never satisfied, never, never satisfied. We can always find something to grouse about. Ah, well!'

'Will you have a drink of something, Father, a glass of lemonade, or a glass of milk? You'd hardly take a cup of tay on a day like that.'

The priest held his hand up.

'Nothing now, Mrs Coyle, thanks very much, all the same. I'm just after two big mugfuls of aleplant there over across. Man dear, but it's wonderful stuff that, isn't it?'

'It's a thing that you hardly ever see nowadays, Father,' Macklin said.

'It is, that's true. I've never seen it anywhere else myself. I had to come down to the Mill Row for it. But here, the old woman's the girl can make it. Troth she can! I don't know what she puts in it, but whatever it is it's good.'

'How did you find her the day, Father?'

'Ah, now, sure what way do you always find her? Working away, working away like a good one. Though,' he frowned slightly and looked down at his hand, pinching thumb and forefinger together, 'I don't think, d'you know, that she looks quite as well as she used to. I know that her heart isn't just what it should be either.'

'Oh, she's been attending the doctor this donkey's years. Father,' Kitty told him. 'But sure, you might as well be whistling jigs to a milestone as talking to that woman. She has herself worked off the face of the earth. D'you know what I've seen that woman doing, Father? Plattering in and out of the yard in the wettest days in winter, with nothing on but a pair of ould slippers, and her fiddling about with her ould buckets, trying to catch some rainwater, and the best of it was, Father, to wash things that maybe had been washed only a few days before.'

'Ah, now,' the priest sighed, 'she's a wonderful old woman altogether, a wonderful old woman.'

'Why don't you come on round, Father, and have a seat?' Malachey invited.

'Lord bless us, Malachey, but would you believe it, I'm tired sitting? I'm wore out sitting down.'

'Come on, on round, Father, for goodness' sake,' Kitty entreated. 'If anyone comes in, they'll think us terrible ignorant people, keeping a priest standing in the hall.'

Father Toner held up his hand again.

'Now I won't sit down, Mrs Coyle, thanks very much. I just dropped in for a minute; nobody'll pass any remarks now.' He turned to Jim Macklin. 'Well, Jim,' he said, 'I hear you have got a big score coming off on Sunday. Sure everywhere I go, that's all I can hear, the big bullet match, Jim Macklin and the Hammer-man! Well, do you think you can win?'

'I'll do my best anyway, Father.'

'I believe he's very good, this Hammer-man. He's coming from Belfast, isn't he? Well, now, it's up to you, Jim, don't let the old Row down. I'm sure there'll be many a bet on you.'

'Well, tell us this now, Malachey. I wanted specially to ask. Is there any word about Paddy and Johnny Kelly? They should be nearly coming home by now.'

'They're supposed to be coming back the night, Father.'

'The night!' The priest's face lit up. 'Do you tell us that? Well, well, isn't that great? I'm glad to hear that. Poor Pachy and Johnny.'

'Two quare artists them,' Kitty commented drily.

'Ah, now, God help them, they were all right,' the priest went on. 'There was devil the happorth wrong with them; a bit on the wild side, that's all. Many a time I passed them coming along on their ould donkey and cart. So they're coming back the night? Well, well, well, I'm glad to hear it, I'm glad to hear it.'

At that moment a scuffle was heard outside the door, and Neilly came bursting in from the street. Shemie came running in after him, half crying. Neilly was shouting: 'A pennyworth of caramels, quick!' as he came in, but when he saw the priest, he stopped dead. Behind him, Shemie stopped too. Neilly was carrying a towel, and both their faces looked pink and clean, with their hair all tousled up.

'Ah, sure; here's the two hardy men themselves,' Father Toner said. 'Have you been bathing? Isn't that grand. And can you swim yet?'

'I can swim, Father,' Kitty spoke up, 'because that same fellow is in the water summer and winter, with clothes and without clothes.'

Shemie hung his head sniffling, and the priest put his fingers under his chin.

'What's wrong, Shemie son?'

Shemie's tears rushed out faster.

'Father, that fellow there stole a penny on me.'

'I did not, Father,' Neilly denied instantly. 'I never stole it on him. He was tossing his penny up at the Corner there, and let it fall on the ground.'

'Well?' the priest questioned.

'Father, he wouldn't lift it up again.'

'He wouldn't lift it up again? Why, Shemie, what was wrong?'

'Father, somebody told him that the devil had kissed it. That's why.'

'God's truth!' Father Toner gasped in astonishment. 'What! The devil had kissed it? Well, here that's the best one I ever heard in my life. The devil kissed it when it was lying on the ground! Well, here, that's the best one I ever heard. But you didn't mind him kissing it, Neilly, eh?'

'No, Father.'

'You thought you could still get a few caramels with it just the same, devil or no devil.' He looked around him laughing. 'Lord bless us, that's the best laugh I've had this week.' He put his hand in his pocket. 'Here, Shemie son, dry your eyes now, and let Neilly keep his ould penny. Here's a new one for you. The devil, I can assure, never went near that one – I hope.'

Shemie wiped his eyes and took the penny shyly.

'What do you say for that?' Kitty prompted sharply.

'Thanks very much, Father.'

'Good man! Good man!'

The two boys bought pennyworths of caramels each, and went out again, leaving the towel lying across the counter. The priest prepared to follow.

'I suppose they're excited about their uncle Pachy coming home again?' he said.

Kitty nodded.

'They have me astray in the mind! Malachey's taking them up the night to meet the train. They're very fond of Pachy.'

'And why shouldn't they be? Why shouldn't they be?' He held his hand up. 'Well, goodbye now. God bless you. I'm sorry to be running away so quick, Mrs Coyle, but I've a few more calls to make before I leave. I haven't been in to see old Liza Taggert yet, and you know how she'd take it if she ever knew there was a priest down in the Row and he leaving without giving her a call.'

'Oh, Lord, surely!' Kitty agreed, smiling. 'You'd never hear the end of it, Father, if you didn't look in on old Liza.'

'Well, good luck now again, Jim, and remember, don't let the old Row down.'

'No, Father.'

The priest went out, and Kitty saw him swing his bicycle away from the window.

'Very nice priest, Father Toner!' Tommy commented.

Kitty stared through the window, watching him throw his leg over the saddle.

'He's a lovely priest,' she murmured. 'There's no one in this town to touch him, a lovely wee man indeed.'

After tea, a crowd of fellows went up to the station to meet the quarter-to-seven train, but there was no sign of Pachy or Johnny Kelly getting off it. The faces of Neilly and Shemie fell.

'There's another train at twenty past eight,' Malachey said. 'We may as well take a walk up the town for a bit. No use going back down to the Row and then having to come up again. You two boys had better clear off home.'

'Oh, Daddy!'

'Oh, Daddy, what? Pachy won't be home the night now. You can't hang around here. Go on now! If they do come the night, you'll see them time enough in the morning.'

The boys trailed disconsolately back to the Row. For most of the evening they hung around the Corner, straining their eyes every so often up the Asylum Hill, seeing in their imagination the familiar swaggering figure coming walking down, with all the fellows; the bright blue eyes, the thin curving lips mocking at the pleasure of coming home. When the fellows finally did come into view, the familiar swaggering figure was not amongst them.

That night, as Neilly lay in bed, he awakened for some reason out of a restless daze. His bed was in the front room upstairs, and as he lay there he heard Pachy's voice outside on the street. For a moment he could not make out where he was; he became confused with that night before St Patrick's Day, in the previous March, when he had lain just like this, listening to Pachy and Johnny Kelly coming into the Row singing. Then his mind cleared, and he jumped out of bed and ran over to the window. He thought that it could not be very late, because some of the downstairs windows on the other side were still lighted. He was just in time to see the figures of Pachy and Johnny Kelly disappear through the door of his own house.

In his excitement, he started knocking at the window, and then rattling it, trying to pull it down. But it was stuck fast. He heard his granny call to him from the wee room downstairs, and he ran to the top of the banisters.

'Granny, Granny, there's my uncle Pachy just home,' he called.

'Go back to bed,' came the old woman's reply. 'You'll have plenty of time in the morning. Go back to bed and don't be standing there.'

Neilly crept back to the window and knelt down, peering out intently at the lighted square opposite, as though, by the concentration of his gaze, he could bore through the yellow blind. Very, very faintly he heard Pachy's deep, humming laugh, and he thought enviously of Shemie, wakening, as he had just wakened, listening, and then creeping down the stairs.

For what seemed ages to him, he knelt there, until he could not fight against the drag of his eyelids any longer. When he rose to go back to bed, the light in the window opposite was still shining.

13

His face twisted in mortal torment, Neilly plumped down the two buckets, just three doors above his granny's. The pain in his shoulders was so great that his eyes watered from it. He looked down at his hands, at the deep, red grooves which the handles of the zinc buckets had crushed into the palms. He looked out dumbly through the film over his eyes.

Failed again!

Then as the pain in his shoulders lessened, he began to wonder why he could not have carried the buckets on down, just that little piece further. Surely he could have clung on for just a little while longer – exerted all his strength? Ah, well, it was too late now. He glanced back towards the Corner; he was getting on, he would do it the next time, definitely, no more codding . . .

Lifting the buckets again, he came on down, and shouldered his way through his granny's half-open door. The old woman came forward to help him, but he kept his grip on the buckets, panting: 'It's all right, it's all right! I'll put them down.' He smiled redly over at Pachy and Johnny Kelly. Teasie had come in, he noticed, with the child; and old Minnie Ryan was still sitting huddled up on the stool beside the fire.

Neilly set the buckets on the form down the hall, with the old woman behind him directing his every move, in case the slightest drop would splash over onto her immaculate tiles.

'Strong man, eh?' Pachy remarked, when Neilly came up again into the kitchen. 'Can you carry them all the way down yet without stopping?'

He and Johnny Kelly were standing against the table, holding cupfuls of the old woman's aleplant. Neither of them seemed to have changed a bit; just the same old Pachy and Johnny.

'I can very nearly,' Neilly answered. 'I carried them two down to Hennessy's door there, and they're far heavier than my mother's were.'

'It's a bad thing to strain yourself, son,' old Minnie quavered. 'You shouldn't go at a thing too hard.'

Old Minnie was a crony of the old woman's, and two or three times a week she would come over and sit down on the wee stool by the fire. The two of them would take out their snuffboxes and start in ridiculing everybody who came into their heads.

'Granny, would you give me a taste of aleplant too?' Neilly asked, and the old woman went down the hall for an extra cup. She moved in between Pachy and Kelly, and lifted out the big glass jar from the window ledge. Pachy noticed again how shrunken the old woman's arms had become, how loosely the skin hung on them.

She filled the cup for Neilly, and then poured what was left into Pachy's and Kelly's. The jar, empty now, save for the three-inch layer of brown, sponge-like plant at the bottom, stood on the table.

'There, you have it all now,' said the old woman. 'I'll have to make some more the morrow.'

Neilly gazed at the rich dark-red juice in his cup. He drank a taste, scringing his teeth against the first, bitter sting.

'If a fellow had a jar of that every day,' Kelly commented, 'the beer could go there.'

Neilly sat down on the edge of the stool beside old Minnie. As his palate grew accustomed to the aleplant, the bitterness faded, and he sipped slowly and jealously.

'Is there anybody at the Corner?' Pachy asked him.

'No, only a couple of young fellows playing handball. All the big fellows are away down the road at the score. Are you going out to the river again?'

Pachy and Johnny had been out bathing with them earlier, before teatime.

'No. Once a day's enough for us, Neilly; we're getting old now, Kelly and me. Got to look after ourselves, you know.'

'You and that river,' the old woman snapped. 'Now sit down. You'll be drownded yet, you and that other wee wasp; he goes in clothes and all.'

'Proper order!' Pachy smiled. 'It keeps you warm that way.'

'There's going to be the quare crowd down that Loughgall Road on Sunday,' old Minnie prophesied suddenly.

'God bless us, it'll be a terror,' Teasie agreed. 'I wonder if Macklin'll win.'

'If he doesn't we're all sunk,' Pachy said. 'I'm putting my Reserve on him, drawing it out the morrow. Then, if he pulls it off' – he shrugged his shoulders – 'fare you well, Killaley.'

'So you'll try England then, Johnny,' Teasie said.

'Ah, sure; what's here for us now, Teasie? Still no word of the ould Mill going on again at all, is there?'

'Don't tell us now, Kelly, for God's sake, that you'd ever go back into that hole?' Pachy said. 'I don't know, to be honest, how people ever work in there. The dust itself is easy enough to give you the jandys.'

'Ah now, jandys or no jandys,' Teasie said, 'it's all right, the ould Mill's all right. The people here, anyway, didn't know they were living, till it went off.'

On the stool, old Minnie cleared her throat carefully.

'I heerd somebody there, the other day, saying that it was going on again next month.'

'Aye, that's right, missus,' Teasie nodded, 'I heard the same thing myself. I trust in God it is. But sure, you mightn't pass on any remarks on anything you hear about the ould Mill. Sure, they have it going on and off every day in the week.'

Pachy shrugged his shoulders.

'Well, I hope it does go on again soon, for the people's sake. The old Bureau won't last for ever. But,' he began scraping his hands together, 'let Macklin win this ould score on Sunday, eh, Kelly? That'll do us.'

'Macklin win?' the old woman retorted. 'H'm! How in hell could that fellow win? Sure he'll have all the throwing threw out of him by the time the score does start.'

'Well, you see, he has to train for it, missus.' Kelly smiled. 'A bullet match is like everything else. You're no good if you don't train.'

'Train, aye!' The old woman would have none of it. 'He'll have himself trained out.'

Pachy laughed.

'You have your aleplant made up, missus, and give him a mugful of it before he starts! That'll put him on his toes.'

Suddenly, and without warning, the old woman turned round upon Neilly. Neilly had moved unconsciously, inch by inch, up the stool until, now, he had old Minnie crushed mercilessly up against the wall of the fireplace.

'Get up out of that, you lazy hulk ye,' his granny shouted, 'with your lying on the ould woman like that. That's every time that woman sits down on that stool, you're crushing and shoving – hell take you! Lie on somebody your own size.'

'Now, leave him alone,' old Minnie panted. 'The child's all right.'

'Run away up to the Corner out of that,' the old woman snarled, 'or sit down right, and do your exercise or something.

'This is Friday,' said Neilly confusedly. 'I don't do any exercise the night.'

'Well, away to the Corner then, with your sitting there looking down people's throats. This is no place for a young fellow like you. Away and get yourself a wee girl, if you want to lie on somebody.'

Scandalised and horrified that such a thing should be said, and Pachy present, Neilly rushed out into the hall. Behind him he heard Pachy call out laughingly, 'Cheerio, Neilly, see you again,' and Teasie's 'God, missus, you're a terror! That was a thing to say to the young fellow.'

Up at the Corner, the boys were still belting the ball up against the rough gable end of the Row. A few others, watching the play, were standing or hunkering against the Asylum wall. Neilly noticed young Vincent Kelly and his dog, Gyp. He had the dog drawn in between his knees, with his hands pressing gently against the mongrel's chest. The dog looked out, regarding the twisting figures of the young handball players, and the black, dancing ball, with unblinking hostile eyes.

Neilly joined the boys silently, his face still burning. As he came over, the dog looked round at him and growled, trying to rise up.

'You'd better take that ould mongler of yours away out of that, Kelly,' Neilly said. 'It bit another young girl last week; I don't want to be the next one. You'll be in for it, if your father sees it up here.'

'My father's down at the score, and it's no mongler,' young Kelly returned. He pressed the dog down gently. 'Good Gyp,' he murmured. 'Lie down now, Gyp, good dog there.'

Neilly looked up.

'Anybody coming round to The Dead again?' he asked.

A great deal of shoulder-wriggling took place.

'It's to coul! The sun's down sure.'

'Ah, I never seen such a pack of coulrifed craythurs in my life,' Neilly blurted.

'Well, away you round, sure. There's nobody stopping you.'

'Ah-h-h-' Neilly picked up a fragment of delph lying at his hand, and began digging it into the ground. Of a sudden, he heard the whirr of a bicycle. Looking up, he saw Eugene speeding towards him on the red, post office bicycle.

Stretching out his hand, Neilly clambered onto the dog as it strained outwards, yelping excitedly.

'I hope that dog doesn't come near me,' Eugene warned. 'It'll be the last he'll ever bite.'

Young Kelly managed to get the dog down between his knees again.

'The bicycle's excited him,' he said. 'You needn't have come up so sudden; sure any dog you meet would bark at that.'

'I'm-m! I'm sure that was all he was looking to do. That dog'll have to be drownded yet, I'm telling you.'

Young Kelly gazed down at the dog.

'I'd like to see anyone trying to drown him,' he muttered sullenly. 'How is it he never bites me?'

Most of the boys had gathered round Eugene's bike. Eugene sat still on it, steadying himself with one foot on the footpath. The boys swarmed around, feeling the tyres, pulling at the brake levers, and thumbing the bell, sending the high, flat, double ring out over the road.

'Eugene, whereabouts are you going?' Neilly asked.

'Moneycree,' said Eugene. 'Are you coming down for a spin?'

The invitation did not have to be repeated!

As they swung away, there came a sudden frantic yowl, and young Kelly's dog came pelting after them. Eugene struggled to get up speed, but the dog caught them easily, and Eugene felt the sharp prod of its teeth on his ankle-bone. Enraged, he kicked out viciously, but the dog evaded his boot and ran in again, its whining bark growing shrill with savagery. Young Kelly raced after them, shouting, and then, as the speed of the bicycle increased, the dog slipped gradually back, still yelping madly.

Eugene screwed round furiously.

'I'll tell your father, you wee skitter ye,' he yelled at young Kelly. 'I'll put the biting out of that thing's head. If your father won't drownd it, I will.'

'Will ye?' The young boy's shout of defiance came back faintly.

Eugene almost choked with rage.

'Aye, I will!' he half-screamed.

'Did it bite you, Eugene?' Neilly asked.

Eugene bent over and rubbed his ankle.

'It got me in the leg,' he said, 'the wicked ould carn. I'll give it the quare boot up the ribs, the next chance I get.'

'It near bit me there, too, Eugene, just before you came down,' said Neilly, not to be outdone, 'only I had a big stone handy, I'm telling you . . .'

They rode on for a while in silence. Neilly gripped the handlebars close to the stem, and lifted his head, eyes narrowed, into the strong breeze blowing past. The oily reek of tar was borne to him suddenly. His nostrils dilated and, as they swept past a loaning, they caught a glimpse of the black boiler a little way down, and the heavy, jaundiced smoke groping upwards from the thin funnel, and the dust, and the men working.

'Did you hear any more word about the accident you had, Eugene?' Neilly asked.

To Eugene the subject was apparently a distasteful one.

'No, not yet,' he said shortly. 'Where's Shemie?'

'Shemie? I dunno. He must be down the road with the score. We should be meeting them soon.'

'It's well for you two,' said Eugene. 'You're getting your holidays next week, aren't you?'

Neilly chuckled and tightened his hands about the handlebars.

'Powerful!' he grinned.

'I wish I was back at school again,' Eugene muttered. 'Nothing to worry about; six weeks' holidays!'

'Slow down!' Neilly cried, pointing, 'there's the score.'

Eugene cautioned him to mind his fingers with the brakes,

stopped the bicycle, and Neilly slid off. The bullet cut past, and Eugene pushed the bicycle up against the hedge.

'Phew! Look at that shot! Macklin threw that, I bet you.'

Neilly laughed delightedly.

'Boy, the poor Hammer-man won't have a look-in. There's Shemie now, look, and my father and Tommy.'

It was Macklin's partner who had thrown the shot, and the two of them, together with Malachey and Tommy, were coming up together. Shemie came running over, and Eugene caught his father's look.

One of the opposing throwers was preparing for his shot, and the two of them, together with Malachey and Tommy, were coming up together. The bullet came slicing up, very fast, but badly played, and about forty yards up it dipped inwards, tearing and slashing through the grass at the side of the road.

As they came walking past, Malachey called to Neilly: 'Where did you come from ? Did that fellow take you down on his bike?'

Neilly nodded uncertainly. His father's face darkened.

He turned to Eugene. 'Will you never learn sense, or are you deliberately trying to get sacked? What would you have done if a policeman had seen you? If you don't want the job, why don't you go up and tell them?'

Eugene lowered his eyes. His father forced his temper down with an effort.

'Go on, for God's sake,' he sighed. 'I don't know what I'm worrying about, it's not my job. I'll always get what'll do me. Go on, run on! You're more to be pitied than anything else.'

'Daddy, will I go with him,' Shemie pleaded. 'Neilly got a ride and I didn't.'

'Aye, sure,' Malachey said, 'the two of you get on there and you might pick up another couple on your way down. Surely, away you go.'

Blushing deeply, Eugene put his foot on the pedal and swung away. Shemie stepped back indignantly.

'Ah, Daddy, look at him! He wouldn't give me one. Ould selfish!' he shouted, but Eugene pedalled on, not turning.

The men walked on and the boys followed. Macklin and his partner were well ahead now, and, as they came up to their mark, Macklin peeled off his coat and gave it to Malachey to hold. He lifted the bullet and, as he threw it, as it swung from his hand, soaring through the air and then flashing down the centre of the road, a deep sigh went up, a murmur of acclaim, wonder and exultation. Roll on Sunday! The Hammer-man was for it this time . . .

14

The big match was due to start at two-thirty, and by two o'clock a great concourse of people had gathered round the Corner, at the Bridge wall. Such a crowd had never been seen at any score before.

The Row was vibrant with excitement. Every door was open, with heads craning out, and here and there women stood along the footpaths, arms folded, gazing up towards the Corner, laughing and chattering. The weather was almost ideal, except for a little sun shower passing now and then overhead, with the steam curling up from the hot road after it had gone.

Macklin stood relaxed against the Bridge, with his hands in his pockets, smiling and talking quietly. The Hammer-man was taller and older than Macklin, and slim. He was so called because of the great strength and power he put behind his bullets when throwing. His proper name was Quinn, and he had arrived from Belfast the night before, staying in a friend's house up the town. The majority of his supporters had followed him on early that morning, in time for ten o'clock Mass in the cathedral. He wore a grey, loosely cut tweed overcoat, a yellow, spotted silk scarf, and a green hat with a large gaudy feather in it. Thick black sidelocks grew down his cheeks.

Malachey Coyle and a little, dark, sharp-faced Belfast man were in charge of the books, standing up against the Bridge wall, the crowd milling about them, with Pachy and Johnny Kelly trying to keep them back in some sort of order.

'Stand back there. Holy God, give them a chance. Stand back. You'll all get on.'

Neilly and his companions crushed about on their usual quest. The musical sing-song twang of the Belfast man stuck strangely on their ears.

Finally the books were closed at a figure never before equalled within memory of the oldest man present. £225 a side!

The throwers peeled off their coats. A coin was spun; the first shot went to the Hammer-man, and to mark the starting butt a handful of grass was flung down onto the road.

The Hammer-man's arms were brown and hairy, with great blue veins; there was a large scar on his right wrist. Lazily he picked up the bullet and walked back a few paces with downcast eyes. He approached the butt in a peculiar manner. His body was crouched low, and he came up warily, slowly, on the tops of his toes, as though he were stalking something. Fifty yards down, his marker stood on the road, his hands on his knees.

Just at that moment, the never-failing scream came from over the Asylum wall, The Hammer-man stopped, and all the Belfast men looked up startled.

'Come on, throw,' the Row fellows laughed. 'It's all right. Half past two! We're dead-on. Throw away!'

The Hammer-man said nothing. He walked back again, his eyes narrowed.

At the butt, the Hammer-man sprang into the air as if he had been shot. All his strength went into the throw. His face convulsed, he gave a grasping grunt, and the bullet left his hand like a rocket. For a hundred yards it drummed at terrific speed along the road. Then it curved towards the footpath. A warning cry rang out, and those on the footpath scattered like blown chaff. The bullet mounted the path and skimmed along like a living thing. Then, without touching the wall, it left the footpath, slicing viciously down the road again. Finally it trickled to a halt, and sat dead in the very centre of the road. It was a magnificent shot of over three hundred yards.

A soft murmur came from the crowd. To mark the shot, another tussock of grass was flung down. In two stages, the bullet was thrown back to the Bridge wall.

Macklin's arms were astonishingly white, but, as he bent down and lifted the bullet, clenching it, the muscles under the skin stood out long and strong. With the sun still shining, another shower swished briefly up the road, but no one paid the slightest attention. All eyes were fixed on Macklin, with a deep hush falling as he walked back for his run. In movement he was sharp and precise, like a soldier on the parade ground. He ran lightly and gracefully to the grass butt, and threw easily, with none of Quinn's exertion.

With a sharp crack the bullet struck the road and sped down the centre, sending up a thin film of spray. It passed through the marker's straddled legs, and dwindled to a faint speck. Gradually it lost its speed, but clung to the dead centre of the road, as though caught in a groove. Finally, it rolled wearily into the grassy slough. A moment, and then the shout came up: 'Hund bullet!'

The next two shots, round a long slow bend, gave Quinn an even greater lead.

At the butts, Quinn would hurl the bullet from him with savage ferocity. The sinews of his neck would bulge, and his face would flush and swell. Each time his bullet struck the road, it seemed that the force of the blow would shatter it into fragments.

Macklin played his shots easily and unhurriedly, always making sure that he had a firm, sure hold on the bullet. He ran to the butts swiftly, but without effort; his leap and throw held a polished grace that was hypnotic. He breathed easily and noiselessly through his nose.

It being Sunday, the road was pretty clear of traffic, but sometimes a car or a bicycle would pass, the tyres hissing sibilantly over some of the wet patches on the road. Men from cottages along the way joined the crowd. The road was soon black with people.

Two miles out, at Allan's stone, roughly the halfway mark, Macklin was one shot behind. Then suddenly another shower broke, heavier than any yet. The road, here, ran through a clump of beech trees, and the crowd scuttled for cover, crowding in under the trees and in against the heavy green hedges. For ten minutes the rain hissed down, and the crowd stared out silently, watching it breaking against the black road, and the sunlight still running over the far fields. Then, as suddenly as it had begun, the rain stopped, and the sun came streaming down through the trees. Everything glittered, and the men came out onto the streaming road, slapping the raindrops off their coats and hats. A car whizzed past, and they drew aside, looking after it.

All the Row fellows began hunching up their shoulders and clapping their hands together.

'Now, Jim, let's cut out the codding and get down to business. Show us what the ould Row's made of.'

Macklin smiled. Then his face set, and those near him could see the little muscles at the corners of his jaws pulsing in and out. As he walked back for his run, he spat on his hands, and at this a wild excitement possessed his supporters.

'Now you'll see something!' they called. 'Belt her out of ye, Jim boy. Belt her out of ye!'

A few of them, however, shook their heads gravely.

'Ah! But all the same – a shot out – a shot out!'

The road swept along in a gentle incline. Fifty yards up, and it flowed around a corner. Quinn was away around this corner, leading by his shot – about two hundred yards. The road was bounded by low hedges, and thin gleaming puddles lay on the surface.

Macklin played the shot with all the skill he possessed. The bullet whizzed up the road, beating a sharp tattoo on the surface. It skimmed the corner, and crossed the road in a long oblique line. Smacking against the low cribben, it spun into the centre of the road, still travelling very fast, and passed Quinn's second-last mark by about thirty yards. Macklin's supporters cheered. A grand shot! A powerful shot! Now for the fireworks.

Quinn, up above, threw a nice shot of about two hundred yards down a dipping hollow. Macklin sent out one of about the same length. Two more shots were thrown by each man, without either making much of it.

For a time Quinn held his own then, losing only a few feet. Gradually, Macklin, with deadly, inexorable shots, began to gnaw away his rival's lead. Excitement grew like a wind-fanned flame. Quinn began to lose his arrogant smile. Sometimes, when one of his supporters spoke to him, he would wave his arm irritably, frowning. He was tiring. His jump no longer held its own elasticity. His breathing became heavy, and a lock of oily black hair fell over his forehead, slapping against it every time he ran to the butt.

With still a mile to go, his lead was reduced to about a hundred yards.

Then the bullet was lost in a thick hedgerow. For twenty minutes they hunted for it in the wild wet grass. The delay seemed to irritate Quinn immensely. He walked up and down, biting his lips. When at length the bullet was recovered, he snatched it, scowling.

Then he made two marvellous shots, actually increasing his lead by ten yards more. His brow cleared, and he began to laugh and joke as before. A gloom descended over Macklin's supporters again. Only a little over half a mile to go. About three shots left to each man. Three shots, and over a hundred yards to pull up! Oh! It was hopeless, hopeless.

A hundred and fifty yards ahead of Quinn the road swirled round in an extremely sharp right-hand bend. Quinn's friends began advising him on the play of the shot. He'd have to watch himself. That corner was almost a right angle. Quinn smiled indulgently, without speaking. He nodded as if he were humouring a crowd of children.

He threw, grinding his teeth, and putting behind the bullet all the strength left in his flaming sinews. His plan was to cut the bullet through the grass at the corner, so giving himself as much clearance as possible, and relying upon the terrific power of the throw to make up for the deadening effect of the grass. The aim was beautiful. Every eye was on the bullet as it hurtled along. It slashed through the grass like a scythe, but its very speed was its undoing.

The crowd shouted and scattered as they saw what was going to happen. The bullet left the grass like a juggernaut, and sliced across the road. It smashed into the wall of the footpath, knocking a lump out of it. Then it leapt back across the road, tore up the ditch and was throttled. Everybody began shouting and swinging their arms.

Quinn came up, frowning with vexation. Then his face cleared. He nodded. Never mind. It would be all right. There was enough clearance for a good shot next time.

Macklin's shot brought him just to the beginning of the corner. A gasp of dismay went up. Faced with the task of negotiating that murderous bend, it seemed that only a miracle could help Macklin now.

Then Quinn made a great mistake. He became too confident. With an ostentatious yawn, he picked up the bullet, trying to impress the onlookers. With an assumed, leisurely indifference, he trotted to the butt and, just as he swung his arm for the throw, he slipped on the greasy road. He staggered, and the bullet, held for a fraction of a second too long, soared into the air, climbing like a bird. It crashed back onto the road, fifty yards down, and ran listlessly for another fifty. Then it trickled into the ditch.

The crowd went berserk. They whistled, shrieked, leaped about and tossed their hats into the air. For half a minute there was pandemonium. Then a great hush came down, as Macklin lifted the bullet. He looked at the corner. Then at the hedge on the right. This was very thick and about seven feet tall. For half a minute he looked at it. His face was composed and grave. Then, without speaking, he walked onto the footpath, pressing up the little grassy bank, crushing in against the opposite hedge as far as he could go. The crowd looked at him in astonishment. Then realisation dawned upon them, and they caught their breaths. Malachey Coyle looked at him.

'You're taking a terrible chance, Jim,' he said.

Macklin spat on his hands.

'It's a chance I'll have to take, Malachey,' he answered quietly.

For a moment he stood perfectly upright. Then his shoulders slumped, and he spread his left hand out. He gave a little hop back onto the footpath, and ran a few steps onto the road. As he threw, a look of agony spread over his face.

A great sigh went up as the bullet left his hand. It swung up, over the hedge on the other side of the road, over the corner of the field, and back onto the road again, cutting the corner completely. It crashed onto the road and sped down the very centre, coming to a halt exactly level with Quinn's butt. Had it been played in the usual way, it could not possibly have come within fifty yards of it.

Macklin's supporters went into ecstasies. They shouted and cheered like drunken men. It was the greatest shot that had ever been seen along this road. It was a shot that would be talked and argued over for years after. Macklin laughed protestingly against the numerous claps raised on his back.

Slightly stunned, Quinn suddenly realised that he stood in dire danger of losing. Up till now, the possibility had never dawned on him. He felt dimly a sense of being cheated. Grimly he threw again. Macklin followed, and again a great shout went up.

'Even butts!'

Excitement burst into a kind of wild intoxication, a frenzied abandonment. Faces flushed; eyes shone. Old men danced about, slapping each other on the back and cackling. But when Quinn lifted the bullet, the scene became as silent as the interior of a great cathedral.

The sun was now beating full on the wet road. The glare cut Quinn's eyes, and he covered them with his hand, waiting. A cloud came past and dimmed the glittering road. Quinn squared his shoulders.

The road swept down, in a slight decline, to the Cabra crossroads, three hundred yards away, and the finishing point of the match. Looking down, a great weariness descended upon Quinn. For the first time he became fully aware of the burning ache in his arms and shoulders. Then he smiled slowly, sure of himself again. It was a cinch! No one had ever beaten him in a straight shot yet. The match was over!

He threw, conscripting from his aching sinews the last ounce of strength, and hurling the bullet from him in one mighty cumulative effort. It leapt down the centre of the road. It dipped once towards the cribben, cushed off again, and ran slashing through a chain of small puddles. It stopped about fifty yards from the crossroads. Casting a superior smile all around, Quinn dusted his hands and donned his coat.

Coming up behind the score on their bicycles, Neilly and the rest of the boys at last became infected with some of the crowd's excitement.

'There must be something good on,' one of them cried, 'who's winning, mister?'

But no one heard him. The boys tried to crush up, but were too late. The crowd was so dense that a dog could hardly have squeezed through.

Up above, Macklin walked back for a longer run than usual. Malachey put his hand on his shoulder.

'That's a terrible shot to have to beat, Jim. But good luck, good luck.'

Macklin gave him a little strained smile. For the first time the calmness and repose of his face rippled. Doubt, anxiety, fear, stood out clearly, but only for a moment. Then his features resumed their masklike expression.

His shot struck the road a little off centre, and a low groan went up. Travelling at an immense rate, the bullet sang down the road. But it gradually sank towards the cribben. Macklin watched. His face was impassive, emotionless, but his hands were clenched so tightly that the knuckles gleamed like naked bone.

The bullet struck the cribben and glanced into the centre of the road again, still travelling very fast; the crossroads seemed a long way off yet. Still, the bullet clung to the centre of the road. It seemed to have taken on a new lease of life, and in the hearts of Macklin's supporters a faint hope began to flutter.

Then came a great gasp as the bullet sank, striking the cribben again. Then a great roar, as it once more ran into the centre of the road. The roar increased, swelling like thunder from hundreds of parched throats. Everyone surged towards the crossroads.

Still in the centre of the road, the bullet swung along. It was weakening now. The roar burst into even greater volume. It became a frenzied howl, clamouring from hundreds of aching, burning hearts.

Twenty yards from Quinn's butt, the bullet went once more into the kerb. This time it did not glance off, but spun along the gutter, through puddles, over straws, over sodden Bo-peep boxes. Everyone watched it with a deathly fascination.

Ten yards, eight, seven, five; but how agonisingly slow it was now! It struck against a stone and wavered, almost stopping. It rattled hollowly over a grating. An empty cigarette box would have stopped it now, but it dribbled on.

Two hands' breadths in front of Quinn's butt, the bullet halted.

The din became deafening. It swelled like the tumult of a great storm-racked sea. People whistled, screamed, shouted hysterically, and tossed their hats into the air.

Macklin had won!

15

That night, at twelve o'clock, there was still a light in almost every window in the Row; some of the doors even lay open with the yellow gaslight flooding out over the footpaths. The hum of voices could be heard unceasingly, except when drowned by laughter or a song. As an old man, who had won ten shillings on Macklin, said: 'It'll be a long while, and indeed it'll be a long while, before anybody in the Row ever forgets this night.'

It would indeed be a long while before anybody would forget the little shop, packed tight; another crowd clustered around the door outside, and Kitty hauling out the six cases of stout, which her farsightedness and confidence in Macklin's ability had prompted her to lay in; and old Mick Murphy and Jackie sitting on the sofa, playing the melodeons and singing, with everybody joining in.

It would indeed be a long while before Neilly, Shemie or any of the rest of the boys would forget it either. They had all been allowed to stay up late and, until eleven o'clock, had been away out through the dim fields, playing 'magpie show your light' – two of the boys running on, with a flash-lamp, and the others hunting the elusive, intermittent gleam, exulting in the lateness and strangeness of the hour. Now, however, they were back, and the crowd of them were sitting huddled on the stairs out of the way, peeping through the banisters and sipping at their free glasses of lemonade.

It would indeed be a long while before anybody would ever forget old Mock Murphy singing 'The Old Bog Road'. A song had ended. When the clapping had died down, Pachy said to Mick: 'Well, give us your ould favourite there, Mick, "The Old Bog Road".'

Then a hush fell, for everyone knew that Mick reserved this song for very great occasions only. If he could be pressed into it now, a treat was in store for all.

Old Mick hesitated at first. Then, with everybody shouting and pleading at him, he at last held up his hand, and everyone shouted 'Hush!' Old Mick started to sing, the music of the melodeons coming in softly.

> My feet are here on Broadway,
> This blessed harvest morn,
> But oh, the ache that's in them,
> For the land where I was born;
> My weary hands are blistered,
> From work in cold and heat,
> But, oh, to swing a scythe today
> Through fields of golden wheat.
> If I could choose to wander back
> Or own a king's abode,
> 'Tis soon I'd see, that hawthorn tree,
> Down the old bog road.

'Good man there, Mick! Good man there!'

Moved by the words of the haunting lovely air, everyone stared sadly at the floor, old Mick's powerful voice hummed through the kitchen; Neilly could feel the vibration of it where he sat on the stairs. As old Mick started the next verse, his eyes were curiously moist, and his face had a strange look of exaltation about it.

> My father died last springtime,
> When Irish fields were green.
> The neighbours said her waking was
> The finest ever seen.

There were snowdrops and primroses,
Piled up beside her bed,
And Fearn's church was crowded
When the funeral Mass was said.
But here I was on Broadway,
A-building bricks by load,
When they carried out her coffin,
Down the old bog road.

To everyone's astonishment, old Mick suddenly gave a loud sob, and his head fell on his chest. He sat there, his big powerful body drooping, and knuckling the tears from his eyes.

'I can't do any more, boys,' he mumbled, 'it's vexed me – it's vexed me –'

Everybody shouted, cheered and clapped, and Pachy emptied another bottle of stout for him, bending the old man's fingers around the glass, as though he were a child.

'Never mind, Mick, that was grand, that was lovely! There'll never be anybody to sing that song like you – "The Old Bog Road".'

Then Pachy had made a speech.

'Well, boys,' he began. And the girls shouted, 'What about us, Pachy?'

'Well, boys,' he gestured towards Kelly and his half-empty glass, 'I suppose you all know that Kelly and I mightn't be with you for much longer. You all know how things are, not a lot of work, and not much sign of old Bessie over there going on again. I hear some talk about it though, and well, I hope for the sake of everyone living here that she will start up soon. But I don't mind telling you that she's seen the last of me, and I'm sure I can say the same for the hard and the wild Kelly here as well. Yes! That day, over seven years ago now, I'm sure many of you remember me when I was working up there in No. 4 – yes, that day when I looked up, and seen the ould dust flying round me, and when I went and threw the ould coat on, and took a walk to myself up Barrack Hill, to see if they were looking for any soldiers. Yes, that day I says, "Right! That's the last of that!" When I said that, I meant it, believe me. So off I went to Indi'. But I never forgot about the ould Row, or about the ould Mill either, bad and all as it was. Many a time out there I lay down and had a blinking good cry to myself. I'm not ashamed to admit it, but well – Yes, the ould Row's all right; many a good one it has turned out on grazed bread and tay. Jim Macklin there, for instance,' (loud cheers) 'and I can tell you this, without fear of any man, that anywhere I ever go, if I hear one ill word said against it, that fellow, let it be the king himself, he'll have to answer to me.'

Everybody clapped loudly and ironically.

'Hear, hear, Pachy. Good man there!'

Pachy took a mouthful of stout.

'Well, so and so, and so and so! But as long as I'm in the chair I might as well take this opportunity of telling Jim Macklin here, and I'm sure you'll all agree, that never again in the length and breadth of Ireland will there ever be another bullet-thrower his equal, except maybe Finn McCool himself, Cuchullain or somebody like that. But all codding aside, that score you threw the day, Jim, I don't think I'm far from wrong when I say that the like of it will never be seen again. The Hammer-man was good, Jim, but he just wasn't good enough. When the return match comes off, I know we can all depend on you to repeat the dose.'

Pachy raised his foam-ringed glass.

'Well, here's wishing you all the best, Jim. We're happy men here tonight, but you're the happiest of us all, because you're the one we have to thank for it.'

As Pachy turned away, the din was deafening. The sudden explosion of sound was so great that one would have thought it would have split the little kitchen open. Clapping madly like the rest,

Neilly juked through the banisters. He caught a glimpse of Pachy's face. It was flushed and triumphant, the blue eyes glinting with tears.

The next instant he saw that a slight commotion had started over by the armchairs, where his granny was sitting. He rose up. He saw his granny huddled in the chair, her eyes closed, her face drawn with pain. Someone rushed down the hall and came back with a tinful of water. Neilly saw Teasie take the tin and tilt it against the old woman's lips. The old woman's eyes flickered and she pushed the tin away.

'Stand out there, for God's sake!' Teasie cried, 'and let the woman draw her breath. No, she's all right I think, Kitty, it was only the heat and the noise and all. Are you all right, missus? Here, take another wee sup of water.'

The old woman shook her head again.

'No. I'm all right. I'm all right.'

Tommy smiled to make light of his sudden fear.

'Are you sure you're OK, Mother? My God, that was a nice shock to give us. I know there'd have been plenty of us fainting if Macklin had lost the score, but nobody should faint now. There, are you sure you're all right?'

The old woman smiled.

'She's not a bit the worse,' Teasie said. 'I'll take her on over. Will you come on over and go to bed, missus? It's far too late for you, anyway. I'll make you a cup of tea. Come on! Now there's no use in you coming as well, Tommy. You stay where you are. We'll be all right.'

She came back in half an hour or so, just when the crowd was beginning to break up.

'She's as right as rain,' she announced. 'I left her sleeping sound. The woman was dead beat, that's all.'

'Teasie, will I go over there the night?' Neilly asked.

'Aye, surely! That's what she said, in fact – 'Tell Neilly to come on over, he'll never be able to get up for school in the morning.'

'Ah, I don't care,' Neilly said, yawning. 'Holidays next week, ha, ha, ha!'

'Well, go in easy now, like a good boy, and don't waken your granny up. With the help of God she'll be all right again in the morning.'

As Neilly crossed the darkening street, he heard someone walking up the Row, whistling 'The Old Bog Road'. Four lines of the song floated through his mind:

> My granny died last springtime,
> When Irish fields were green.
> The neighbours said her waking was
> The finest ever seen.

Of a sudden he realised his mistake and as he stepped up on the cribben on his granny's side, he halted, a dreadful coldness closing slowly around his heart.

The old woman's recovery was not so speedy as Teasie had prophesied. She lay for three days, and Teasie stayed with her on Monday and Tuesday nights. Neilly lay with Tommy, not that the old woman gave any serious cause for alarm, but just in case she might wake up in the middle of the night wanting something.

Father Toner came down to see her, and said jokingly that he was glad to see her having a bit of sense at last, and taking a rest.

She ate little, but drank a cup of tea sometimes, with a pinch of ground ginger in it. She never touched loaf bread, and complained of the farls which Teasie baked, saying that there was enough soda in them to kill an army.

Pachy and Johnny Kelly were leaving on Wednesday evening, and she got up to see them off, saying what a pity it was that she hadn't a fresh drop of aleplant to drink their health in.

'You take care of yourself now, missus,' Pachy laughed, 'and you can brew some up and send it after us. When they get the taste of it over there, we might be able to get you some orders in, and you can start up here on your own.'

Malachey, Tommy and the two boys accompanied them up the Row. Kelly had dropped a note to his sister, and they were crossing to Liverpool and thence on up to London. Pachy had done a good bit of travelling before, so they would not be at any handicap in that respect.

As they walked up the Row, every head was out, with Pachy waving his hand and shouting out farewell remarks. A big crowd of fellows had gathered at the Corner. Pachy cast down one long last look, and then the whole bunch of them moved on up the Asylum Hill. Kelly walked along, as quiet as ever, but Pachy seemed to be in the best of spirits, laughing and joking about how, in a year or so, they'd be coming back again in a Rolls Royce, and another one coming behind with their luggage.

At Mann's public house, at the station, they went in for a farewell bottle. Glasses of grapefruit were handed to Neilly and Shemie. They sipped at it suspiciously, for it was the first they had ever tasted, running their teeth over the tiny grape shreds.

'I'm drunk,' Shemie whispered to Neilly, 'I can feel my head going round.'

Malachy paid for the drinks, and Pachy wanted to call for some more.

'Fill them up again there, Paddy,' he said to the barman. 'Christ the night! I'll never get a bottle like that where we're going.'

But Malachey was frightened lest another round might lead to still another, and there would be no Pachy or Kelly on the boat the night, so he winked at Tommy and then suddenly everyone had had enough, and look at the time it was anyway; they'd have to run for it as it was, never mind having another drink!'

On the platform, as the train came in, and everybody began clearing their throats, Shemie suddenly went into a violent fit of weeping, with Neilly, half crying himself, sneering at him and telling him not to be an old woman. Malachey lifted him up, and Pachy petted him out through the carriage window and pressed a shilling into each of the boy's hands, telling them to be careful and not spend it all at once, for that would have to do them till he came back again; by then he'd have enough money to buy them a bicycle apiece, and maybe a pony as well – just for a change, you know. Then the train was moving, and Neilly's heart clashed with a sudden inrush of terror and a pain such as he never felt before. He stood still, with his mouth as dry as stone, wanting to turn, and run, and run, until all sight and sound of the train, and Shemie's screams, had died behind him.

Now that the old woman was up, neither Tommy, Teasie nor Kitty, even, could get her back to bed again.

'I'm all right,' she said. 'I'm going to wash that delph on the shelves up there; it's bogging. And I'll have to bake some farls of my own, quick. That bread, that you and Kitty makes, would have me in my coffin before the end of the week.'

They gave her up in despair. Neilly moved back into his bed in the front room. He lay in bed, that night, staring out through the window. In the warm darkness, he could just make out the shape of the roof opposite.

It did not seem possible that Pachy could be gone; he couldn't think of the Row without him. The thought of getting his holidays on Friday no longer meant anything to him, nor did he feel any gladness at being back in his granny's again, or at she being all right. Pachy was gone!

He didn't feel like this when Pachy had been going to prison; it had been different then somehow – different – But now . . .

He raised himself on to his elbow, and in a sudden, awful, heart-searing flash he knew that, in spite of what Pachy had said to him, he was never going to see him again.

16

As the two boys were getting over the stile onto the straight road beyond, Eugene came whizzing round the corner of the Asylum Hill. When he saw his brothers, he jammed his back brake full on and screeched in beside them.

He put one foot on the stile – Eugene never dismounted unless it was absolutely unavoidable.

'What's the river like,' he asked, 'any good? It should be warm the day; I'm sweltering in this blinking uniform.'

He was carrying his cap in his hand, and his shirt was unbuttoned, with the collar out over his tunic. His sun-flushed face, and the exposed skin of his chest, was gleaming with perspiration.

'Oh, it's powerful, Eugene,' Shemie told him eagerly. 'We're coming back again. It would roast you, wouldn't it, Neilly?'

'Many out?'

'It's packed! You missed the gaff; the Preacher got threw in.'

Eugene swung his leg off.

'I think I'll take a race round; it's early yet. My father's not there, is he?'

'He was round earlier on, him and ould Mick Murphy,' Neilly said, 'but I think they went away for a walk somewhere.'

'I got powerful news the day,' Eugene smiled. 'D'you mind thon accident I had? Well, it's all over at last. And boy, am I glad?'

'Why, what happened?'

'Ah, an old Surveyor's Caution came through for me the way from Belfast. What do I care? I had a good idea I wouldn't have got the sack anyway. I hope it'll stop all this casting up from my father.'

'What's a Surveyor's Caution, Eugene?' Shemie asked.

'A Surveyor's Caution! Well, it's a caution from the Postmaster-Surveyor in Belfast. You see, it comes on paper; then you sign it and hand it back. Three of them's supposed to get you the sack, but I don't care.' He laughed. 'I can get another one yet.' He took Neilly's towel, and gave him the bicycle to bring round. 'Tell my mother I won't be long. Here, you might as well bring my cap round as well; it might roll in.'

He hopped over the stile, and the boys watched him racing up the loaning, swinging the towel. Neilly set the cap on the back of his head, and sticking one leg through the frame of the bicycle he pushed off unsteadily.

'I'm a telegram boy,' he shouted. 'Mind out there! Telegram for you, mister, telegram; you've won the Sweep.'

Shemie caught hold of the back mudguard and raced after him, shouting that he wanted to be a telegram boy too. Neilly screwed around tormentedly.

'Let go, let go, you'll throw me off, and the bike'll be wrecked. Let go, and I'll take you round from the Corner.'

Shemie relaxed his grip, but he still ran on, keeping up with Neilly, determined not to be cheated.

Just before they got to the Corner, a boy and a dog came round. Neilly recognised young Vincent Kelly and Gyp. He saw that young Kelly was crying, and stopped the bicycle and came over. The dog commenced its low, ugly snarl, and he eyed it uncertainly.

'What happened, Vincent?' he asked. 'I thought you were round at the river.'

Young Kelly knuckled his eyes.

'My father – my father says that I have to drownd Gyp,' he blubbered.

'Why, what's wrong? Did he bite somebody else?'

'He bit my father,' the boy wept.

'Oh, my God!' cried Neilly. 'It's for the high jump this time all right.'

Young Kelly leant against the rough gable, his face turned inwards, his shoulders shaking with sobs and hiccups. The dog sat back on its haunches, at his feet, its little inimical eyes fixed on Neilly, the ugly growl still vibrating in its throat. For almost half a minute no one spoke again. Then Neilly ventured: 'Well, look, Vincent, what are you going to do then? If you're going to drownd him, what are you going to drownd him with?'

No answer!

Neilly fidgeted.

'Well, will I come with you then?'

A muffled 'I don't care!'

'Will I get you a piece of rope?'

No reply save a painful groan.

'Shemie, will you take the bike on down, and see if you can get thon ould piece of rope that's lying in the yard. Here, take the cap as well.'

Shemie took the cap and balanced it on his ears, grinning. He pushed on down the Row, with one foot on the pedal of the bicycle.

Neilly came over cautiously and stood beside Vincent. He twisted his hands behind his back.

'Don't be crying, Vincent, sure you can get another ould dog somewhere. I'll get my uncle Tommy to get you another ould dog somewhere. Don't be crying.'

They walked abreast across the field, heading for the red iron gate in the far corner. The dog slouched behind them. A length of thick, ban cord was tied around its neck and clasped in young Kelly's right hand. His chin hung on his chest as he walked. He never glanced up, or paid the slightest attention to his companions. A terrible dejection was apparent in every line of his slender body. His eyes were inflamed from weeping, and the grimy remnants of his tears streaked his pale cheeks. A length of rope hung over his shoulder.

Shemie kept throwing swift darting glances back and forth from the mongrel to Vincent's tear-stained face; his eyes were dancing with excitement and wonder.

The boy had not spoken since they had started out, and indeed seemed oblivious to all that had been said. Suddenly he flung his head up. His voice, as he spoke, was filled with anguish and desperation.

'Well, I don't care! I don't care,' he cried. 'I'm not going to drown him. I don't care what my father says. I don't care. I'm not going to drown him –'

Silence for a few steps, and then Neilly pressed.

'Well, and what are you going to do with him then, Vincent? I don't want to drown poor old Gyp either, but sure, if you let him off, you know he'll come back, and I'm telling you I wouldn't like to be facing your father then.'

At that moment they reached the gate. Shemie and he climbed, the bolts rattling and clanking in their loose sockets. Vincent plunged into apathy again, ducked listlessly through the bars, dragging Gyp after him.

On the other side, they stood in a group looking down at the dog. It gazed up at them quietly, for once.

'My God! Would you look at it now, would you?' Neilly grunted. 'You'd think that butter wouldn't melt in its mouth, to look at it sitting there. I bet you it's sitting there just aching to get sinking its teeth into one of our legs.'

Shemie gave a startled giggle, and took a couple of quick hops backward. Young Kelly looked up sourly.

'Ah, what are you hopping about, spider?' he growled. 'You don't think he'd bite a little blert like you? And you needn't be casting up at him, Neilly, either. I never seen him doing you any harm, so I never.'

He and the dog moved out across the field. After a moment Neilly and Shemie followed quickly.

The field through which they now walked was very large, and sloped gradually down to the silver curve of a river about a quarter of a mile away. Dozens of small sand-coloured haystacks were dotted haphazardly about; the after-grass had the dark, cool green of water-weed.

'My God, Vincent,' Neilly broke out again, 'your father must have been in a terrible crab!'

Young Kelly's eyes flashed.

'Ah, sure, it's not Gyp's fault, is it?' His voice was clotted with rage, and he shouted the words as thought to someone a long distance away. 'It's them little yaaps of girls that keep tormenting him.' His voice broke into a sob, and he looked over at Neilly appealingly. 'I don't know what everybody is blaming Gyp for,' he almost wept. 'You never saw him biting me, did you?'

'Ah, it's all right talking like that,' Neilly said relentlessly. 'But sure he has bit dozens and dozens of people, and sure they weren't all girls, and sure they weren't all tormenting him.'

Silence again for a while. Then Neilly went on softly: 'Ah, sure, Vincent, it's the only thing. He'd only be getting your father summonsed. Then he'd only have to be shot, anyway.'

'I knew a dog like that,' Shemie burst out eagerly, 'a dog like Gyp; always went about biting the people, and he had to be shot. The police came down,' he rushed on, warming to his subject, 'in a big black van, dozens and dozens with machine guns and rifles and all, for this was supposed to be a terrible dog, and one of the cops got his arm tore off and another one –'

'Oh, for God's sake, what are you telling us a yarn like that for?' Neilly interrupted, disgustedly.

He and Shemie kept arguing as they walked on, but Vincent

paid no heed. His shoulders and head were bowed. He walked like an old man.

When the boys came to the river, they halted on the very edge of the bank, and stood gazing down into the water. The bank was about fifty feet high, where they stood, and the river about fifty feet wide. The water moved along like thin oil, slow and deeply silent. Only in the drift of a leaf, or a yellow straw, upon the dark surface, was its motion perceptible at all, Out in the middle, a fish jabbed up, and the faint concentric ripples beat slowly out, ever-widening and ever-fading.

Behind the boys, Gyp, as he sat on the grass, dug his snout into his shoulder, searching for a flea. The faint click of his teeth sounded clearly in the stillness of the afternoon. The boys turned. Shemie stretched his arm forward, snapping his fingers.

'Here, Gyp,' he called, 'good boy. Good boy!'

Gyp did not respond very favourably to his advances. He rose up, lips peeling in a churlish snarl. Shemie laughed uneasily.

'Aha! Look at that, look at that! And I never touched him either. Oh, bad Gyp.'

Young Kelly stepped over, his face bitter.

'There you are, you little spider ye. What am I only after saying? You're fiddling round it there, and if you got bit, you'd be the first to run whingeing to my father about it. How is it he never bites me? That's what I'd like to know. How is it he never bites me?'

Bending down, he began caressing Gyp's head gently. He swept back the long ragged ears, slitting the little eyes.

'There you are,' he repeated sadly. 'Does he bite me now? Does he?' He rose up slowly. 'If you would only leave him alone.'

For almost a minute they stood in silence looking down at the dog. Then suddenly, Neilly turned his head away.

'Well, there's no use standing here all night, sure. We might as well get it over with.'

The young boy trembled, and began to rub his hands together as though it had suddenly become very cold.

'Neilly,' he burst out tearfully, 'you do it, will you? You do it –'

Neilly looked at him.

'All right, if you want me to.' He moved away from the bank. 'The first thing we need, well, is a big stone, a big, big stone.'

Thirty yards away was a cows' drinking place. The banks were trampled down to the water level. In the wet weather, this place was a gluey morass, but now it was quite firm, the imprints of the cattle's hooves baked hard by the sun. Neilly and Shemie walked down, and a few cows retreated uneasily, the water swinging from their thick pale lips. The boys selected a large stone sealed into the ground, and, after a great deal of straining, they succeeded in wrenching it up and carried it back to the four-foot bank. Neilly wiped his hands on the grass and lifted the rope which Vincent had dropped from his shoulder. He tied one end of it securely around the stone, and then straightened up and looked down at the dog.

'I don't know how we're going to get him tied,' he said.

'Be sure, well, and keep a good hold on him. I'm not looking for the hands to be tore off me.'

Lifting the loose end of the rope, he approached Gyp warily. The dog crouched back, his jagged snarl oozing slowly. After a slight hesitation young Kelly bent and caught him, holding him tightly and murmuring to him. Gyp yelped bitterly, as the rope went round his neck, and lunged so fiercely that the young boy could hardly hold him. Shemie danced about, almost beside himself with excitement.

Neilly knotted the rope as quickly as he could, but just as he stepped away, a final, murderous lurch momentarily freed Gyp from young Kelly's hold. The boy made a grab at his hind leg. Gyp slewed round, straining and yelping viciously. Neilly retreated, his left wrist scratched and bleeding.

'Curse that ould mongrel of yours anyway, Kelly,' he ground out bitterly. 'It should have been done away with long years ago.'

But the other was conscious only of a surging exultation. The world was all against them. It was only right that Gyp should strike back in return!

Neilly ran his tongue over his wrist. The scratches were only superficial, but they smarted painfully. Scowling, he rolled the stone over till it lay on the very edge of the bank. He called to Shemie, telling him to be ready to push the stone over the moment he shouted. Then he gripped the rope (the slack was about four feet long) and began hauling Gyp forward.

The dog braced his forelegs against the ground and strained its head up, yowling frantically, but inexorably it was dragged closer to the river. Young Kelly's heart burned as he watched. Tears ran down his cheeks. He sobbed wildly, gnawing at his wrist and striking his right foot against the ground.

Then suddenly, Neilly shouted to Shemie, and there came a plumping splash as the rock hit the river. The next instant, with a yelp of bewildered terror, Gyp was snatched awkwardly over the edge of the bank. The three boys rushed forward and peered down into the river. Its smooth surface was shattered, and beneath the twisting frills of water, young Kelly, with smarting eyes, thought he could make out the body of the dog in writhing distortion.

'Oh Gyp! Oh Gyp!' he moaned, over and over. The next moment, as if resurrected from the riverbed by the force and intensity of the young boy's anguish, the dog's head rose above the surface. It was whining and breathing gruffly.

Thunderstruck, the boys stood still. Then Neilly shouted: 'Get back. Get back! The rope's slipped. We're ruined.'

He and Shemie skipped back, but young Kelly was struck motionless. He stood like one in a dream.

Crazed with rage and hate, Gyp spun round in the water. Then he came heading for the bank. He clawed frenziedly up onto the field again, and hurled himself upon young Kelly. The boy fell, with the dog on top. Suddenly terrified out of his daze, he tried to beat it off, but the dog lunged in, driving savagely for his throat. The scrabbling claws tore at him. He began screaming.

Neilly rushed over and swung his boot. He caught the dog in the throat and he tumbled over, coughing harshly. Before he could recover, Neilly gripped it by the hind legs and, exerting all his strength, slung Gyp far out over the river.

Gyp struck the water, a misshapen bundle. He sank, but reappeared instantly, his eyes bulging madly. Neilly began stamping desperately at the edge of the bank. He succeeded in loosening a large lump of earth and, raising it dripping above him, he brought it down with all his strength on the dog's head.

Gyp disappeared about a dozen feet from the bank. He came up looking dazed and weak. His snout was plastered with mud, and his paws flapped blindly at the water. Neilly bent down and loosened another sod. Slowly and deliberately he aimed it. With back-breaking force it crashed down squarely on Gyp. The dog sank. A big bubble welled up and broke. Then a second and a third. The pieces of grass which had gathered on the surface slowly drifted away. The muddy stain in the water gradually faded. The river became smooth and dark again.

For a long time, without speaking, the boys stood staring down into the water.

Young Kelly's hands and knees were torn and threaded with blood; blood oozed slowly from a claw mark on his cheek. Now and then he would look down at his hands or reach up slowly and touch his scratched face, as though unable to grasp the reality of the wounds.

At length Neilly raised his head. He noticed, for the first time, the blood on the other's face, hands and knees. Shemie and he moved over, hissing as they examined the wounds, and then advising the boy to come home at once and have them bandaged. But young Kelly paid no heed. He still stood looking down at the river. He did not seem to hear his friends, or even to be aware of their presence.

Neilly moved away a few steps and Shemie followed. Neilly turned, and called impatiently: 'Come on, on out of that!'

But young Kelly did not look up. His eyes, as he gazed down into the river, were filled with many emotions: remorse, fear, sorrow, bewilderment, perplexity.

His face had the look of a person struggling with some vast, insoluble mystery . . .

17

When Neilly got back to his granny's, about seven o'clock, he found a small crowd of women gathered in the kitchen. As he closed the door behind him, Teasie came out of the small room.

'Here's Neilly now,' she said, as she saw him. 'What kept you so late?' Before he had time to reply, she went on: 'Look, son, your poor granny has had an accident, and she's back in bed again. She's worried wondering where you were. Go on in and see her.'

Neilly looked round him dazedly. He noticed his mother among the women.

'Is that Shemie fellow back as well?' she asked him, and just as she spoke, the door opened softly and Shemie came in, his face pale.

'Go on in, the two of you,' Teasie said, pressing open the door of the small room. 'Go on.'

Tommy looked round as the boys entered. He was standing at the head of the bed by the little table against the window. One hand was resting on the table, the other on his hip. His right leg, crossed over his left, was knocking softly to and fro in a nervous habit he had. He lifted his hand from his hip and gestured.

'Come on over,' he whispered. 'Don't shout, your poor granny's not well.'

'Is that Neilly?' the old woman cried, in a pain-stricken voice. 'Is that you, Neilly? Come over here. Where were you till this hour? Is that Shemie, too? I thought the both of you had fell into the water this time. That Shemie fellow's be drownded yet.'

The old woman's faded grey eyes were glazed over with pain, and her lips were tinted blue. The two boys stood awkwardly at the side of the bed, their arms stretched straight down.

'We were round drowning Vincent Kelly's dog,' Neilly said. 'It bit Vincent's father, and it had to be drownded.'

A pained smile plucked at the old woman's lips.

'God's truth!' she whispered. 'That's a good one – Bit Kelly himself? He'll not bum much about that. Did you drown it all right?'

'The rope slipped the first time, Granny,' Shemie put in excitedly, 'and it came up again. Vincent Kelly was all scrabs where it turned on him. Then Neilly caught it and threw it back in again, and got it right on the top of the head with a big sod, oh, a lovely one!'

The old woman tut-tutted faintly.

'You might have been all ate alive. That dog was a wicked carn. I'm glad to hear the last of it.'

Neilly looked round at Tommy. He was gazing at his mother, steadily taking in every movement of her head and every word she spoke. He caught Neilly's glance and smiled, pursing up his lips, his leg still shaking.

'What sort of an accident did you have, Granny?' Shemie asked. 'Did you hurt yourself?'

The old woman raised her wasted arm tiredly, and let it fall back upon the quilt. Neilly noticed the heavy veins beneath the brown, crinkled, shiny skin.

'The ould delph!' she said. 'My back's near broke. I was taking the ould delph down to give it a wee wash, and the next minute . . . hah, delph, chair and all – ah, now don't be talking – and me lying in there amongst them. "Where's Neilly?" says I, "and his poor old granny lying here not fit to move." But Neilly was out round the river somewhere, sporting himself.'

The tears sprang to Neilly's eyes.

'Granny, if I had a knew I'd a come round, wouldn't we, Shemie? We'd have lifted you up –'

'But Neilly and Shemie didn't seem to care about their old granny at all, or what way she was lying there, and all the lovely delph, and the plate with the big blue ring round it; it was a bit chipped, but what about it? I had that plate a long time, ah – oh – And there wasn't a tint of water down the hall to wash up the dishes in, and Neilly said he would get me a go from the pump. But Neilly couldn't be found anywhere, and not a tint of water was there in the house, and me lying there gasping for a drink – and my poor back.'

'Granny, I don't know,' Neilly cried out in agony, 'Shemie and me would have run round, but we didn't know, sure.' The tears squeezed from his eyes, and his hands clutched at the heavy bed quilt. 'Granny, I'll get you a go of water now, if you like, will I? And I'll carry it all the way round.'

'I never liked chairs,' the old woman was whispering. 'They're the curse of God.'

'Don't be crying, Neilly,' Tommy said, 'she doesn't mean anything. Her mind is wandering a bit,' he said to Teasie, who had just come in. 'Neilly's crying because she said he wouldn't bring her a go of water.'

'Ah, God help him!' Teasie murmured. 'Dry your eyes, son, and don't pass any remarks. Her mind is a wee bit dazzled. Come on, on into the kitchen, and come you out too, Tom; let her rest, the doctor'll be down any minute now.'

She put her hand to her breast.

'As true as God's in heaven, I'm not the better of it yet,' she declared to the others. 'When I walked in and seen that woman lying there on the floor, I thought I was sent for. That woman, you know, should never have been up at all, but sure you could never tell her anything.'

The hum and swish of a car sounded outside, and Teasie rushed towards the door. The doctor came in. He was a young, thin-faced man, with his short, crinkly once-black hair now almost completely grey. A blue beard-shadow was stamped underneath his pale skin.

Teasie showed him into the small room, describing what had happened, and he crossed the kitchen silently, not looking at anyone.

When he came out again, he stood by the door for a moment, frowning morosely.

Everyone in the kitchen looked at him. He lifted his head.

'Well, she's had a very severe shock,' he said to Tommy. 'She has been very lucky in respect of physical injuries. Her back has had a bit of a wrench, and there's a nasty bruise over her hip, but no bones have been broken, which is very remarkable for an old woman like that.'

While he was speaking he kept rubbing the forefinger and thumb of his right hand together. He spoke carefully and deliberately, enunciating each word as though it was of inestimable value.

'The main danger is from shock, and she should be kept as quiet as possible, and given plenty of hot drinks.'

His gaze moved slowly from Tommy to Teasie.

'Mrs Coyle's heart, as you know, is not any too sound, and a shock like that could easily prove fatal. It was a great mistake that the woman should have been allowed out of her bed in the first place.'

Teasie said nothing, hypnotised by the smooth, dispassionate flow of words.

'Where is the lad who came up for me? Ah, there you are.'

Eugene had come in shortly after him.

'Will you follow me up again? I'll let you have a prescription for some ointment and embrocation. I'll drop down tomorrow again myself. Remember now, she must be kept as quiet as possible.'

Teasie left him to the door again, and he went out without another word. The car turned and rolled up the Row, with Eugene following on his bike.

'He's a queer client that, what?' Tommy was saying, as Teasie closed the door again and came in.

'Never smiles!' Teasie said. 'Never smiles at all. I never seen him smiling in my life. But he's a good doctor all the same.'

'Well, here, come on, you two, and I'll get you your tays,' Kitty directed the boys.

They hung back, and Teasie said: 'Ah, let them stay there, sure I'll make them a drop.'

'Indeed, you'll do nothing of the sort! You've enough to do. I'll learn them no such habit. They should have been in for their tays at the proper time.' Kitty ushered them into the hall. 'Come on, over you go! It's the first time I've ever had to force you in for anything where your stomachs were concerned.'

In sudden remembrance, Neilly glanced back at the three shelves of delph above the sofa. He had not noticed, as he came in, but now he saw that the bottom shelf was almost empty. The three lovely little ornamental cups that hung from the hooks were gone, too.

That night, Neilly moved back in with Tommy and Teasie slept in Neilly's bed in the front room.

At the beginning of the week, when the old woman had first taken bad, she had told Teasie to put the child in with her. This had been her practice before Teasie and Tommy had shifted, because she was very fond of the child. Teasie had humoured her, and that night as well the granny and the child slept together in the wee room. The next day she seemed bravely, screwing up her nose at the reek of the embrocation, and joking about the broken delph, with Teasie saying: 'Well, missus, I'd rather that it was you nor me, for if anyone else had broken that delph they'd have had to have left the country.'

On Sunday night, though, she seemed restless, and Teasie, in spite of her objections, removed the child, thinking that it was disturbing her. During the night, Teasie rose twice, but the old woman appeared quite at ease and sleeping soundly.

The next morning a great change seemed to have taken place. She lay on her back in the bed as though in a coma, her eyes half closed and the breath husling between her parted, bluish lips. Teasie went for Tommy, and he came in and stood staring stupidly down at her. Teasie lifted up the child and showed it to her, asking if she'd like it in with her for a while. When the old woman did not recognise the child, Teasie felt within her that it was the end.

She told Tommy to go over for Kitty. She came in with another woman, by the name of Mrs Cousins. When she set her eyes on the old woman, her first words were: 'You'd better send for the priest, Tommy, for that woman's going.'

Tommy laughed at her in derision. Oh, not at all, don't talk silly! His mother dying! Nonsense!

But Father Toner was got, and he came down and administered the Last Sacrament.

Neilly and Shemie had been sent out earlier on, without anyone telling them anything, and they were sitting on the Bridge wall when a young girl came round the Corner shouting: 'Neilly Coyle and Shemie, you are a-wanted! Your granny's dead!'

When the boys got round, they found Tommy sitting with his arms and head on the table in the kitchen, crying hoarsely. As they came in he raised his eyes to Neilly's horror-stricken face.

'Neilly, Neilly,' he shouted, 'd'you know what's happened? Your poor granny's dead. Oh, Christ, Jesus, your poor granny's dead.'

During the time of the wake and the burial, Tommy remained in a hopeless condition; no one could do anything with him. On Monday morning, the day after the old woman's death, he suddenly disappeared, and no one knew where he had gone. About four in the afternoon there was still no sign of him. Malachey put on his coat, and took a walk up the town. About an hour later a car drew into the Row, and Malachey helped Tommy out. Tommy was so drunk that he wasn't able to stand.

Sickened and scandalised, Teasie put him to bed upstairs where Neilly had slept. About two o'clock in the morning he came slowly down into the crowded kitchen, eyes filled with the nausea of living.

Teasie came forward in the silence, to assist him to a chair, but he walked on without speaking, into the room where his mother was laid out. Teasie's feelings towards him were more of anger than anything else.

'Why doesn't he try to pull himself together?' she said to Kitty, who was present, 'and not have everybody talking about him, going about drinking at a time like this, and sitting in there like a wee child, crying.'

Finally she went in and tried to reason with him, but he rose up in a sudden rage and pushed her out.

'Leave me alone. For God's sake, leave me alone,' he shouted. 'What do I care about the people, or you either? There's the only one I ever cared for, lying there. Go to hell from about me; if it wasn't for you, she might be alive still. The ould doll wasn't good enough for you; you couldn't wait to get away from her. Well, you're far enough away from me, too. I got drunk the day, yes. And I'll get drunk every cursed-well day from now on, and let whoever the hell dares, say one word to me. You needn't start your hushing, Kitty; you're just as bad as the rest of them. Every bit!'

He caught a glimpse of Neilly's frightened face peering through the banisters – Shemie had been carried out asleep, long ago.

'There's the only kid who ever thought anything about the ould doll, the only kid in the house. Many a go of water he brought for his granny, didn't you, Neilly? Many a time I was here, when he came in and asked his granny if she wanted a taste of water.'

He walked over and sat down on the stairs beside Neilly, and put his arm around him.

'The only kid in the house!' The tears were trickling down his cheeks. 'Neilly, your granny was fond of you.' Suddenly he buried his face in his hands. 'Oh, what am I going to do?' he moaned, his body swaying to and fro. 'God, Christ, Jesus! This is fearsome.'

After the funeral the next day, he disappeared again. This time

Malachey and Jim Macklin were hot on his trail, and managed to get him before he had had too much.

'Malachey,' he sobbed, 'she's gone now, the best ould craythur – but the ould house is still there, and if I'm living and spared, back into it I'll go. That's what killed her, Malachey. She was never the same woman after we left: I've never spent a happy hour in that ould barrack of Kelly's. Back into her house I'm going to go. But sure it's too late, it's too late. She's dead . . .'

The three of them moved slowly down the street, with the passersby glancing curiously at Tommy's unsteady gait, and haggard, grief-striken face.

18

The water struck the clay barricade across the sheugh, and swirled around as if bewildered by the sudden obstruction. Then it deepened and crept very slowly out onto the road, reaching for the end of the dam. Shemie watched it until it was about to dribble round the end. Then, with an exultant cry, he slapped down another handful of earth, cutting off the water's escape.

A frenzy took possession of the boys. Savagely they pulled at the bank, tearing lumps out of it, with a sound like that of cloth being rent. They made the dam thicker and higher, bringing it out onto the road in a gentle, inward curve. Shemie muttered and laughed to himself as he worked. He worked as though charged with a sacred duty, as if some fearful disaster would occur if the water were allowed to break free.

Racing out of the houses and down the road, after the cessation of the rain, which had fallen, heavy and implacable, all day, the boys had been unable to resist the sight of the swift-flowing sheugh water. All day they had been cooped up in their houses, but now the misery of those hours were forgotten. Their bare feet made wet, slapping sounds on the road, and the backs of their jerseys grew speckled with tiny pinpoints of water, cast up by their prancing feet. Now and then one of them yelled; a wild, unintelligible shout of joy, that pierced through the hum and clatter of the Mill beyond.

After about ten minutes they stood up, breathing heavily, with flushed faces. The water had swelled into a little lagoon, but it was yellow-coloured now, no longer clear, and around the dam the yellow deepened to the darker colour of the clay. Beyond the dam the sheugh was barren, empty.

The boys stood looking down at their handiwork. The sunshine drove through a rent in the heavy black clouds that were still moving across the sky, and the light splashed upon the water, and lit up the long, wet grass on the bank above.

'Come on, and we'll build another one further down,' Neilly suggested, 'and then we'll let this one out. Shemie, you stay here and keep watch on that one, will you?'

Neilly and the rest of the boys moved on down the road about twenty yards, and started pulling and stamping more sods from the bank. Shemie stood with his hands behind his back contemplating them. Then, smiling faintly, he looked down at the dam he had been left to mind.

The water was brimming; soon it would spill over. Yet Shemie did not move. He looked down again at the boys below, engrossed in what they were doing. Cautiously, Shemie put his foot out, and with his big toe scraped a groove in the top of the dam. A thin trickle of water ran over. He scraped again, a little deeper. The trickle widened, scurrying down the empty channels on the other side of the dam. Shemie's mouth opened. Then, with a gasp, he bent down, tearing fiercely at the dam with both hands.

A thick, glossy mane of water leaped through, and rushed down the sheugh, sweeping pieces of the burst dam with it in the energy of its release.

Fascinated, Shemie watched it go. He saw it get to within a few feet of his brother. Then the boys, hearing the gurgle behind them, swung round. Before they even had time to be surprised, the water had hurled itself upon their unfinished blockade, snarling around their naked ankles. The dam crumbled, the water sweeping it contemptuously aside and racing on in its newfound freedom, a swift, yellow streak.

The boys looked at their ruined dam, with a slightly bewildered air, as if they could not comprehend the suddenness of what had happened. Then Neilly saw Shemie looking down at them, smiling. His face twisted and he rushed up.

Instantly Shemie bent down and picked up a large stone off the ground. He flung his arm back, poised for a throw.

'Don't come any nearer,' he shouted, 'or I'll cut your head off. I'm not codding now!'

'If you hit me with that stone,' Neilly yelled, 'I'll give you such a thump – What did you let the water out for, you bad-hearted wee blert? You'll never come out with us again.'

He took another step. Shemie fired the stone at him and took to his heels. The stone went wild, and Neilly sprinted after him and gave him a dig in the side with his left hand. Shemie staggered in against the bank; his bare feet slipped in the muddy sheugh, and he fell full-length on his back into the water.

He clambered up again frantically, as if the water was boiling hot. A howl of unutterable dismay burst from his lips. He stood up in the sheugh, holding his arms out from his sides.

'Now, look what you've done,' he bawled. 'Maybe you're satisfied now. Ah, mammy!'

All the boys gathered round him. Neilly licked his lips.

'Ah, quit your shouting,' he said, 'that's what you get! It's nobody's fault but your own.'

Shemie turned his head round, feeling the back of his trousers and jersey.

'I'm wriging,' he moaned. 'Oh, mammy! Look at all that muck; it'll never come off.'

He rushed at Neilly in a fury.

'It's all your fault,' he screamed, 'you dirty big bully ye. You're always fighting.'

Neilly caught him by the arms.

'Quit it,' he shouted desperately, 'quit it, or I will hit you. You want to get dried, don't you? Come on, on round to Teasie's. Teasie'll dry you, and Tommy'll soon be out.'

The rain was starting to spit again, and suddenly it came down with a rush, beating up a white blur from the road.

'Come on, run for it!' Neilly yelled, and they tore back up again, with the wind swinging the warm rain in against their faces.

As they reached the Corner, the screech of the Mill whistle burst forth, and Neilly dragged Shemie in against the Dining Room door.

'Wait,' he panted, 'there's the Mill off. Wait, and Tommy'll be out.'

Up above, the big wooden gate rolled across, and a crowd of men and women rushed forth onto the road. Some of them turned up the Asylum Hill and others hurried round towards the Row. Neilly caught a glimpse of Tommy, coming round with his head down, one hand holding onto his cap, and the other drawing the lapels of his jacket over his chest.

Neilly grabbed Shemie's hand and raced over.

'Tommy! Tommy! Will you take this fellow down and dry him? He fell into the sheugh.'

'He pushed me in, Tommy,' Shemie groaned.

Tommy came to a startled halt.

'What? What's wrong?' Then he added: 'Come on then, get down quick out of the rain. Run!'

The three of them burst into the house breathlessly. Teasie looked round from the fire, with the teapot and kettle in her hands.

'What's wrong?' she frowned. 'What's all the rush about?'

In the wee room the child was sitting propped in the pram, knocking an old celluloid rattle against the sides. As the boys and Tommy came in, the child stopped, and gazed at them with a thin thread of saliva running from the wet, open mouth.

Tommy took off his old tow-flecked jacket and hung it up behind the door.

'Nothing's wrong,' he smiled, 'it's raining.'

'In the name of God,' Teasie ejaculated, as she caught sight of Shemie, 'have you fell into the river again? Isn't it wet enough for you out on the bank?'

She set the teapot and kettle back on the hob, came across and ran her hand over Shemie's trousers and jersey.

'Look at the state of you with muck! You needn't go home like that, Kitty'll take your sacred life.' She glanced out through the window. 'Did she see you come in? You're a terrible wee fellow altogether! What were you doing?'

Shemie started to cry again.

'I wasn't doing anything. That fellow pushed me into the sheugh down the road.'

'Who pushed you into the sheugh, you wee liar ye?' Neilly cried hotly. 'I didn't push him into any sheugh. He slipped.'

'There's no use in starting to cry again, Shemie,' Tommy said. 'Teasie, you'd better see if you can get them ould clothes off quick, and get them dried. Kitty'll be out roaring in a minute. Go on, carry on; I'll attend to the tay part.' He started to pour the boiling water into the tea. 'Will I fill it up?' he asked.

'Aye, fill it up,' said Teasie.

She spread a double sheet of newspaper on the ground by the fire.

'Here, son, stand on that and get them ould things off. They'll not be long a-drying in that blaze.'

'Look at all that muck, Teasie!' Shemie quavered.

'Ah, that'll brush off the best, son, as soon as it's dry. Hurry up now, you boy ye, and I'll get you an ould coat to pull over you.'

Shemie's eyes were fixed on the door of the shop across the street. The door was closed, but just as he was unbuttoning the neck of his jersey, he saw it swing open, and his mother lean out over the half-door. She turned her face up towards the Corner, and her shout came to him shrill and urgent.

'Hi-i-i-i, Neilly! Hi-i-i-i, Shemie!'

Shemie stood petrified. Kitty shouted again and then, as she withdrew, and the door closed over again, Shemie, with all the speed at his command, began to strip off.

'You're in luck,' Teasie commented, 'she hasn't seen you come in.'

She took Shemie's jersey, semmit and trousers and hung them over the upended stool. She threw an old showerproof on the sofa and handed Shemie a towel.

'Here, give yourself a bit of a rub with that first,' she said.

As Shemie was drying himself, he saw Neilly smiling at him out of the corner of his eye and lashed out with his towel.

'Who d'you think you're grinning at?'

'You needn't laugh now, Neilly,' Teasie said. 'It's not the first time I've seen you in your skin either. What were you doing, anyway, that you pushed him into the sheugh?'

'I'm telling you I didn't push him into the sheugh,' Neilly protested indignantly. 'I gave him a good dig, that he deserved for wrecking the dam, and he slipped into the ould sheugh. He's a poor wee craythur; he never does anything.'

Tommy had poured his tea, and was sitting down on the armchair. He held the teapot over Teasie's cup.

'Do you want your tea now, girl?' he asked.

'Wait a minute, Tom. Set it on the hob there. What dam are you talking about?'

'Och, you know; a wee dam across the sheugh.'

Tommy poured some milk into his cup. The milk billowed like a cloud through the rich, dark tea. Tommy looked at it interestedly, watching the creamy swirls creeping like tentacles through the cup;

then he stirred, and the colour of the tea lightened to a uniform dark brown.

'What's all this damming?' he said. 'There's no call for cursing sure.'

'We're not cursing,' Neilly emphasised. 'I don't mean that kind of dam. You know, when you build something to keep water out – ah, go on! You're smiling; you know rightly.'

'There's your mother out again,' Teasie said suddenly. 'Maybe I'd better call over and tell her you're here. She must be wondering what's happened.'

But Shemie rose up from the sofa in fear.

'No, Teasie! No, don't! Wait'll my trousers dry.'

Kitty's shout came again.

'The woman'll be astray in the mind,' Teasie said.

Looking through the window they all saw Kitty turn and gaze directly across. It seemed to Shemie that she was looking straight at him. He slid off the sofa, and juked behind the stool over which his clothes were drying. Then his heart gave a great leap. Neilly and Teasie called out: 'Here, she's coming.'

He looked up and saw Kitty halfway across the street, holding an old coat over her head.

'Oh, Teasie, save me, save me!' he moaned. He started a run to the wee room, the showerproof slipping off him on to the floor, but Teasie caught him, half laughing.

'Stay where you are, for God's sake. You'll be all right.'

The door rattled open and Kitty came in, swinging the old coat off. The first thing that struck her eyes was the bold Shemie, completely naked, squirming in against Teasie trying to hide. She threw her old coat over the end of the banisters.

'Hah!' she said, 'I thought this is where you'd be; I thought so. I knew the minute I let you out of the house the day that you'd go right round and fall in the Callan River.'

'Ach, now, give your head peace, woman dear,' said Teasie, 'he's not a pickle the worse, and there's his clothes there near dry. So you won't have any trouble at all. Here, wrap that ould mantle round you again there, Shemie. If some of your wee girls were to walk in now, you'd be disgraced till the days of amen.'

Kitty looked over at Tommy and shook her head. Then she turned on Neilly.

'And what were you doing, long-back? I thought I told you to mind him.'

'He pushed me in,' Shemie pouted.

'Don't tell tales now, Shemie,' Tommy said.

'I didn't push him in,' Neilly cried. He was getting a bit tired of this. 'I'll put your eye in a sling if you say I pushed you in again,' he shouted at Shemie. 'He slipped in, and it wasn't the river either, it was the sheugh.'

'River or sheugh, wait till I get you over,' Kitty threatened.

'Ah, I don't think you can blame one more than the other, Kitty,' Tommy put in. 'As far as I can make out, they were building an ould dam, or something, across the sheugh down the road, and the tight Shemie here thought it was no good of an ould dam, and that he could build a far better one himself. He wrecked the ould dam, but Neilly here thought, dambut, it wasn't such a bad ould dam after all. So he gave Shemie a welt on the ear, and Shemie slipped and fell into the ould dam.' He paused, laughing, with a cut of jammed bread in his hand. 'Dambut here, what!'

'It wasn't a welt on the ear! It was a big dump in the side,' Shemie scowled.

'You shut up,' snapped Kitty, 'for you're the devil's own torture. It's well seen that you knew where to come, anyway. You were wise enough there.'

Tommy smiled.

'Force of habit, Kitty! When the ould doll was alive, this is where they always made for, when anything happened.'

Kitty put her hand on Shemie's steaming clothes.

'I'd better go over and rout you out an old pair of trousers. You can't sit here in your figure. It'll be ages before they're dry. Oh, God! It'll be the happy day for me when your holidays are over and you're back at school again.'

'Let them sit there,' said Teasie, 'sure what harm are they doing? I'll give them a drop of tay and they can take it in their hands there. What's the hurry? Malachey's over across, isn't he?'

Kitty objected violently; their own tays were sitting on the table ready for them. But Tesaie said: 'Hold your tongue, sure it'll do for their supper.'

She began hacking away at the loaf. The child began to whimper, and Kitty went in and lifted it and sat down on the sofa.

'It can't be hungry,' Teasie remarked, 'for it's had a bottle there just before Tommy came in.'

The boys were handed cups of tea and slices of bread and jam. Then Teasie sat down herself.

'No more word since the last,' Kitty answered. 'Oh, God knows when that fellow'll write again. He never thinks, for God's sake. He mightn't have writ at all even, if he hadn't heard about the ould doll.'

'They didn't stay too long with Eileen's man,' Teasie commented. 'It couldn't have been much of a catch after all.'

'No, they'll be many's a place before they end up, the same pair. Still, I think they're far better on their own, d'you know. They're in some big hotel now. Pachy's doing some kind of cooking. He done a bit of it in the army, you know. Oh! God help the people who have to ate what thon fellow cooks. I don't think they'll get lighting long there!'

Teasie smiled.

'God help them. Kelly and him thought a lot of the ould doll, God rest her soul. Many a good laugh I used to get out of them over there, and, oh, Lord bless us, but the ould woman used to be delighted to see them ateing. Isn't it a strange thing; but she loved to see anybody ateing! Isn't that strange? She used to sit and watch your two men, and she'd be breaking her sides laughing at them. And the aleplant! Lord, but they were dying about their aleplant.'

'Teasie, you know, tried to make some there, Kitty,' Tommy said, 'and by the Lord God it would have killed cats.'

'Ah, get away out of that, it's not that bad,' Teasie defended. 'Neilly had a taste and Shemie there, didn't you, Neilly?'

'What was it like, Neilly?' Tommy asked.

'Ah, it was all right.'

Tommy burst out laughing.

'Well, there's the jar in the window, still full, anyway. It burnt a big hole in the tablecloth the other day.'

'It must have been a terrible shock to Pachy,' Teasie said, 'all the same, the quick way she went, just a loc of days after they left, and her getting up to see them off and all.' Teasie shook her head sadly, eyes narrowed against the steam from the hot tea. 'That was her end, you know, getting up like that. God, she was a terror, and the ould cap; she sure got her money's worth out of that ould cap. I think she slept in it sometimes. Ever since we came back there, d'you know. I can't get used somehow to not seeing her about the house. Sometimes I be sitting here, half-expecting her, you know, to come pattering up the hall from the yard, or in off the street, barging away and the ould cap pulled down over her eyes. God, she was a shocking woman! We fought, her and I, aye, in the house and out of the house, but she was the heart or corn. I mind the day before she died, Sunday! She said to me, I mind it well: "Teasie," she says, "I haven't done very well by you, God knows, but if I ever get over this . . ." And mind you, she seemed rightly that day, didn't she, Tommy? Laughing and joking about the ould delph, and saying that somebody was going to get the quare rip for some more plates, the next time she went up the town.

I laughed then. Ah-oh, I often think, too, how she would have loved to have seen the old Mill going again. She used to love to see Tommy coming in from it at night.'

'Aye,' said Tommy, heavily, 'there'll never be another one like the ould doll. She was one of the real ould stock, they're dying out now.'

'D'you think the ould Mill's going to stay on this time, Tommy?' Kitty asked.

'God knows, Kitty, God knows. Nobody seems to know a thing about it; old Boyd'll say nothing. Still I think it's on for a spell, anyway. They say they left another load of tow in the stores the day again.'

They sat on talking; and then, when Shemie's clothes had dried, Teasie took a knife and scraped the caked mud off. Then she scrubbed them vigorously with a brush till all trace of it had gone.

'Come on now, you,' Kitty directed, 'get them on quick. We can't sit here all night. Your father will be wondering what's up. Thanks be to God, anyway,' she sighed, 'that the school opens again on Monday. I dread these holiday times, especially in weather like this – they're in on the top of you, and you can't get a hand's turn done. Tsk, tsk! Look at that rain, still teeming away. Don't tell us that we're in for another flood again already.'

Kitty handed the child over to Teasie, and shepherded the boys out into the hall.

'You're lucky that you're not going over to your father in the state that you came in here in.'

'Don't say a word to them, now,' Teasie said. 'They're all right. Neilly's the boy slips me in a wee taste of water now and again.'

'And I can carry it round all the way now, Tommy, without stopping.'

'Can you? Good man!'

'Aye, I done it yesterday for the first time – all the way round.'

'Good man!'

'Well,' said Kitty, 'I hope you'll always be so ready with your arms.'

She hoisted the old jacket round her shoulders and pulled the door open.

'Cheerio, now! I think it's going to fair. It's brightening up a bit there over the Asylum. Come on, you, keep well in, under the coat, and mind you don't go plattering into the puddles.'

They rushed out and scurried quickly across the street into the shop.

When the door had closed behind them, the Row was deserted again.

The rain still fell heavily, driving down between the gleaming, chimney-shadowed rooftops, but the darkness in the air was beginning to lift, as a white, glowing patch spread slowly in the sky above the Asylum trees. For a while everything was silent, except for the whisper of the rain and a faint, almost inaudible humming from the now-empty Mill. Then, down towards the bottom of the Row, a door opened and three young girls, standing on chairs, leaned out over the half-door. Their young, happy voices jigged sharply through the street, through the warm, grey evening air:

> Rain, rain, go to Spain; never show your face again.
> Rain, rain, go to Spain; never show your face again.
> Rain, rain, go to Spain; never show your face again.
> Rain, rain, go to Spain; never show your face again.